THE WINDS OF TIME

Chad Oliver

THE WINDS OF TIME

Doubleday & Company, Inc.,
Garden City, New York

This book is fiction,
and all the characters and incidents in it are entirely imaginary.

To CHUCK BEAUMONT and BILL NOLAN
Because the world is like a falcon

THE WINDS OF TIME

chapter 1

THE CABIN WAS A NEAT COMPROMISE. FOR THE MAN, FED UP to the gills with the stinks of the city and afflicted with the annual back-to-nature bug, it had yellow pine walls with prominent rustic knotholes. For the woman, resigned to another season of losing her husband to a series of glassy-eyed trout, it offered an electric refrigerator, moderately efficient gas stove, a shower with hot water, and inner-spring mattresses on the beds.

Weston Chase, pleasantly fueled with ham and eggs and three cups of coffee, had only one immediate aim in life: to get out of the cabin. He sat on the unmade bed and tied the laces of his old tennis shoes, then clapped a stained mouse-colored felt hat on his head and shrugged into a supposedly waterproof jacket. He stuffed chocolate bars and cigarettes into his pockets and picked up his tubular rod case and his trout basket.

Now, if only——

"Will you be long, hon?"

Too late, he thought. Now came the Dialogue. He knew what he would say, and he knew what his wife Joan would say. The whole thing had the massive inevitability of Fate.

"I'll be back as soon as I can, Jo."

"Where are you going?"

"Up the Gunnison, I think. Pretty rough going that way. Sure you wouldn't like to go?"

"Wes, there's nothing to *do* up there."

Weston Chase edged toward the cabin door.

Joan sighed audibly, shoved back her fourth cup of black coffee, and put down the paper with a flourish. (It was the Los Angeles *Times,* which caught up with them two days late.)

"Run along, hon," she said. "Mustn't keep the trout waiting."

He hesitated, smothering his guilt feelings. It *was* sort of a dirty deal for Jo, he supposed. He looked at her. With her blonde hair uncombed and without her make-up on, she was beginning to show the years a little. She had refused to have any children, so she still had her figure, but her good looks were blurring a bit around the edges.

"I'll be back early," he said. "Tonight maybe we can go see Carter and Helen, play poker or bridge or something."

"Okay," Joan said. It was a neutral noise; she was Being a Good Wife, but not pretending to be ecstatic about it.

Wes kissed her briefly. Her mouth tasted of sleep and coffee.

He opened the door, stepped outside, and was a free man.

The thin air was clean and cold, and it hit him like a tonic. It was still early, with the Colorado sun wrestling with the gray morning clouds, and the deep breaths he took tasted of the night and stars and silence. He got the engine of his car running on the third try—the carburetor wasn't adjusted for mountain driving yet—and then switched the heater on.

He pulled out of the Pine Motel drive, vaguely annoyed by the two wagon wheels at the entrance, and drove back through Lake City. Lake City wasn't much to look at but, as always, it

10

filled him with a nameless longing, a half conscious summer wish to get away from the smog and the traffic and settle down in a place where the world was fresh. His eyes told him the truth: Lake City was not precisely a ghost town, but the coffin was ready and the hole was dug. It was just a pale collection of wooden stores and houses at the foot of Slumgullion Pass, kept more or less alive by tourists now that the silver mines were gone. The sign on the road outside of town claimed almost a thousand residents, but most of them must have been of the invisible variety.

But he watched the curls of blue smoke rising in the air and sensed the warmth behind the glass windows of the Chuck Wagon, where a tired girl was putting plates of ham and eggs on an old scarred counter. He saw three oldsters already swapping lies in front of the ramshackle post office, and he was honest enough to envy them their life.

His car hummed out of town, crossed the bridge, and sped into the morning along the Gunnison River. The Gunnison was blue and inviting, framed by snow-capped mountains and bordered by dense green brush and reddish strips of gravel. He opened the window and could hear the icy water chuckling and gurgling by the road. He knew the Gunnison, though; it was swift and deep and rugged. Wes cut off from the main road a mile outside of Lake City and drove over a dirt trail until he came to a small winding creek that tumbled down out of the mountains. He took the car as far as he could, and then parked it in the brush. He opened the door and climbed out.

There was only one sign that a man had ever been in this spot before—an empty, dirt-streaked jar that had held salmon eggs lying by a rock. He had tossed it there himself a week ago.

He smiled, feeling the years fall away like discarded clothing. He felt his heart eager in his chest, and his mind filled with warm, faraway images: a boy shooting tin cans on the Little Miami River in Ohio, building rock-and-clay dams on back

11

yard creeks, snagging a sleepy catfish from a green river island. . . .

He locked the car, gathered up his gear, and hit the path with a long, springy stride. He grinned at a jay squawking across the sky, caught just a glimpse of a doe fading into the brush ahead of him. The path angled upward through a valley of green and gold, choked with grass and flowers, and then climbed along the white-flecked stream into the mountains.

The trail was rough and little used, but he stuck with it. For the most part, he kept the stream on his right, but he had to cross it twice when the rocks and brush cut him off. The water was glacially cold and his tennis shoes squished when he walked. He knew there were trout in the creek, fanning their fins in the ripples and hovering in the black, shaded pools. There were enough of them so that he could count on getting seven or eight if he spent the day at it, and probably two of them would be pretty good rainbows. But today he wanted to do better than that. There was a tiny lake, fed by melting ice, up above timber line, and there the golden native trout were sleek and hungry, far from the hatcheries and the bewildered fish that were dumped into the more accessible streams and caught before they knew where they were.

The lake was almost fourteen thousand feet up, so most of the boys with the fancy equipment left it alone.

Wes climbed steadily, knowing he would be dog-tired before he got back down again, and not caring. His doctor's mind told him his body was in good shape, and he was reassured. The sun was still playing tag with grayish streaks of cloud, but he could feel his face burning a little in the thin air.

Around him, he was aware of magnificent scenery without looking at it directly: cool pines and stands of graceful aspens, their slender white trunks like cream in the sun. A miniature jungle of ferns and hidden insects, and a soft wind rustling through the trees. Once, the mournful cry of a wolf far above him.

12

If only a man could come here and live, he thought. If only he could forget his security and the string of runny noses that were his patients.

And then the trapping whisper of reason: *You'd freeze in the winter, Jo would hate it, where would your kids go to school if you had any kids. . . . ?*

It was eleven o'clock when he got above the timber line, and even the stately spruces were behind him. The path twisted through rocks and dark clumps of brush with startling green leaves. The stream was only some three feet across here, but fast and cold as it rushed with a sibilant *shhhhhhh* down from the lake.

The lake itself, when he finally reached it at twenty minutes past eleven, was nothing much to look at, unless you happened to be a fisherman. It was a flat pond, almost circular, perhaps one hundred and fifty feet across. The sun was almost directly overhead, and the water appeared dark green; the few spots that were rock-shadowed looked black. There was still ice on the peak that rose behind the pool, blinding in the sunlight.

It was as silent as though the world had just been created, fresh and clean and new.

Wes sat down on a rock, shivering a little. He wished the clouds would disperse for good, even though the fishing would be better if the sun weren't too bright. He wasn't tired—that would come later—but he was hungry. He wolfed down two chocolate bars, getting an almond fragment stuck in his teeth as usual, and drank some cold water from the stream where it ran out of the pond.

He slipped his brown fly rod out of its case and stuck it together firmly. He took the black reel from his trout basket and clipped it into place. He squinted at the leader, decided it was okay, and tied on two coachman flies. Probably the salmon eggs would do better in the deep water, but there was plenty of time.

He stood up, lit a cigarette, and maneuvered himself into

13

position: shielded on one side by rocks, but with a clear space behind him for casting.

The world held its breath.

He flicked the flies with an easy wrist motion and they patted the water to his right, only five feet from shore. He left them a moment, two specks of brown and red resting on the green surface of the water. There was a slight wind ripple on the pond; otherwise, all was still.

He tried again, letting out more line and casting straight out in front of him. Nothing. He drew the line back, wiggling the flies in the water——

Strike!

A flash of flame-colored fins, a heavy shadow beneath the surface, and the flies disappeared. The line tautened, the fly rod bent double and jerked with a life of its own.

Wes excitedly muttered a crackling string of choice swear words, directed at nothing in particular, and backed away from the lake. A bad spot to use the net, just toss him out on the rocks——

There! The trout broke water and tried to snag the line on a boulder. Wes kept the line tight, waited until the trout relaxed just a trifle, and heaved.

He had him. The trout flopped on the rocks, the fly worked out of his mouth——

Wes snatched off his hat with his left hand and dived for the fish, clapping the hat over him like a basket. Carefully he reached under the hat, grabbed the trout, and broke its neck with one quick jerk.

He sat on the rocks, grinning idiotically, admiring his catch. It was a nice one—a good fourteen inches, and heavy with firm flesh. Wes popped him in the basket, fastened the buckle, and shook out his line.

"Won't get skunked today," he said, exhilarated out of all proportion to what had happened. What was it about a fish, anyhow, that made him feel like a kid again? The thought died

14

in birth; he didn't care why it made him happy. It *did,* and that was enough.

He advanced on the pond again with a sure instinct that today was his day to shine. He forgot everything: food, rest, promises to Jo. Every atom of his being was concentrated on the trout in the pool. Every fish he caught stimulated him to want more.

For Wes Chase time ceased to exist.

The trout basket grew heavy against his hip.

His wet feet ached, but he didn't feel them.

He noticed the gray clouds that filled up the sky around the mountain peak only because the fishing was even better now that the water was shadowed and restless.

At four o'clock in the afternoon the storm hit with a paralyzing suddenness. He was taken utterly by surprise as the pond before him was instantly transformed into a pitted black mass of excited water. He felt a numbness in his wrist where something icy rested. He looked around, trying to adjust himself to a change that had caught him thoroughly flat-footed.

Hail.

It wasn't rain, but hail—round pelting chunks of ice that seemed to materialize on all sides, blanketing the rocks and plunking into the water. It was very still; there was no wind.

At first he wasn't afraid. He was annoyed, and that was all. He picked his way back to where he had left his rod case, took the rod apart, and put it in the tube. The hail got under his collar, melted, and trickled down his back.

He noticed two things: it was darker than it should have been, and he was cold. His first thought was of shelter, but the unhappy fact was that there wasn't any. He was above the timber line, and there wasn't even a tree to break the hail.

He stood up straight, trying to make as small a target as possible. He wished fervently that his hat had a wider brim on it; he could hear the hail pocking into the felt, and the crown was already getting soggy.

15

He remembered an abandoned miner's cabin back down the trail. Its roof had collapsed, but the four walls were more or less intact, unless his memory was tricking him. No matter—the cabin was a good two miles away, and the hail was so thick he could hardly see the trail.

The storm got worse.

A cutting wind came up, sweeping out of the north, slashing the hail against his face. He stuck his red, numbed hands in his pockets and held the rod case under his arm. He raised his head and looked around almost desperately.

There was nothing. The slick rocks were blanketed with hail, and the world that had seemed so inviting a few hours earlier now presented a bleak aspect indeed. He checked his watch. Four-twenty. It would take him two hours to make the car under the best of conditions, and he wasn't anxious to try that path in the dark. He waited, shivering, but in ten minutes the hail showed no sign at all of letting up.

He turned his back to the wind and managed to get a cigarette going on the fifth match. Then he squinted his eyes and fumbled his way to the path that led along the rushing stream, back down the mountain. He was decidedly miserable, and more than willing to concede that civilization wasn't so bad after all.

It he could just *get* to it.

The hail rattled down with a vengeance, and Wes began to worry about his glasses. If they broke, he would be in a bad fix for following a mountain trail. He tried to keep his head down, but that exposed his neck.

He tried to increase his pace, and promptly slipped on the hailstones and fell on his back. He got up, unhurt but touched by panic.

Slow down, he thought. *Take it easy.*

It was hard to see. He couldn't just follow the stream because the rocks and brush barred his way. If he could remember which side of the stream the path was on——

He couldn't. He floundered along what he had thought was

16

the trail, and it just stopped against a rock wall. The wind was whistling now, the hail the worst he had ever seen. He looked at his watch.

A quarter to five.

It would be dark in an hour unless the clouds lifted.

He tried to retrace his steps and fell again, landing in a clump of wiry brush that scratched his face.

Wouldn't do to bust a leg. No one knows where I am.

He stopped, shielded his eyes, tried to spot something, anything.

There.

Above him.

Was that a rock shelter, that shadow beneath the ledge?

He put down his rod case and trout basket and scrambled up the rocks. He ripped his trouser leg, but he couldn't feel a thing. The stinging hail was right in his face and he lost his hat. He flopped over a ledge—like a fish, he thought wildly—and scrambled into the hollow made by a rock overhang.

The wind still cut at him. He bent over double and squeezed his way toward the back of the rock shelter. He saw an opening—not a big one, but large enough to admit his body.

A cave?

He didn't care what it was.

He took a deep breath, felt ahead to make sure there wasn't a drop, and squirmed inside.

chapter 2

IT WAS TOO DARK FOR HIM TO SEE CLEARLY, BUT IT WAS DRY. He fumbled in his shirt pocket under the jacket, took out a match, and struck it. He held it above his head, trying to make out where he was.

The tiny light didn't do much good. He must be in a cavern of some sort, he reasoned; he could see only one side of it, although the ceiling was within easy reach. Something gleamed with a metallic reflection about fifteen feet behind him—a vein of ore, probably.

The match went out.

He listened, ready to translate the slightest scrabble or scratch into wolves, snakes, or other charming companions. He heard nothing. There was only a hard, dust-covered silence in the cave.

18

He thought: *I may be the first man in the world who has ever been in here.*

Ordinarily, the notion would have given him considerable pleasure; as it was, he was too miserable to be impressed. He was wet, cold, and tired. There was nothing he could make a fire with. Outside, a scant two yards from his head, the storm was cutting loose with an icy, persistent ferocity.

And it was getting dark.

Why didn't I bring a flashlight? He thought of those cheerful cartoon ads in which deep-sea divers, bear hunters, and dauntless young executives were inevitably saved by good reliable flashlight batteries. Suppose you didn't *have* a flashlight? Could you throw the batteries at the enemy?

He laughed, felt a little better, and lit a cigarette. The smoke, at least, was warm. His patients were always asking him about lung cancer, and he always answered them solemnly. Just the same, he stuck to his tobacco.

He made plans, shifting his position to get a sharp rock out of his side. He would stay here all night if he had to; the storm couldn't go on forever. Then get back to the car, drive to the cabin, and tell Jo what had happened. Then a hot shower, breakfast with steaming-hot coffee, and a round of antibiotics from his bag. He had plenty of free samples, fortunately. The drugstore in Lake City was probably still in the blackstrap molasses and yogurt era.

Was his throat already getting raw, or was that imagination? *Physician, heal thyself* . . .

Two cigarettes later and it was six o'clock. Night had fallen outside in the storm, and a deeper blackness crawled inside the cave around him. There was a change in the sound of the storm; he heard a hissing and a gurgling that must mean that the hail had turned to rain. A hard, driving rain. He knew from past experience that the water would be gushing down the mountain trail two or three inches deep. It would make for treacherous going at best. He would never make it at night

19

without a broken fibula or so, and that would be a pretty picnic.

He peeled the paper from a candy bar and ate the chocolate slowly. He decided to save the remaining two for breakfast before he started down the mountain in the morning.

He was already stiff and sore, and he knew that a night on the rock floor of the cavern would do nothing to loosen him up. But he *was* tired. Maybe if he could doze a little the time would pass more quickly.

He twisted around on the rocks to find a more comfortable position and discovered that there *were* no comfortable positions. He wadded up his handkerchief for a pillow and closed his eyes.

The storm roared wetly outside, but it was a steady sound, almost soothing . . .

He slept.

He tossed fitfully on the hard floor of the cave, asleep and yet somehow aware that time was passing. He held on to sleep almost consciously, as though a part of him knew that it was easier than waking up in the cold.

And then, quite suddenly, he was fully, intensely awake.

Something had awakened him.

What?

He lay very still, listening. The rain had stopped, and the world outside was hushed and dripping. Pale moonlight filtered into the cavern, touching it with ghostly silver.

He checked his watch. Two o'clock.

There. A sound: a muffled click, like a metal latch.

It was inside the cave with him.

He held his breath, his aches and pains forgotten. His eyes searched the cave, seeking——

Another sound. A rasping scratch, like a fingernail on a blackboard. From behind him, where the cavern wall glinted a little with a metallic sheen.

An animal?

His eyes tried to pierce the gloom. He could *almost* see in the half-light, but details were fuzzy. He was filled with a nameless, irrational dread. All at once there was no civilization, no science, no knowledge. There was only himself, alone, and a primeval darkness choked with horror.

He rolled over as quietly as he could. He got up on all fours and crawled toward the cave entrance. He put one hand outside, grasping for a hold on the damp rock.

Then he heard it.

It was something *opening.*

He looked back.

Someone—something—was walking out of a hole in the cavern behind him. It was tall—it had to bend over to keep from hitting the roof of the cave. It had a cadaverous face, pasty white. It had eyes——

It saw him.

It came after him.

Wes Chase couldn't think; his mind was paralyzed. But his muscles could act, and did. He threw himself out the cave opening, scrambled down the rock shelter. He listened for the stream, swollen with rain, and ran for it.

He found the stream, almost black in the silver blue of the moonlight. He spotted the trail, a deeper darkness in the rocks. He plunged down it as fast as he could go. He slipped, almost fell, caught himself on some tough strands of brush.

Slow down, he thought. *You'll kill yourself.*

He looked back over his shoulder. He saw only a pale lunar world. He heard nothing but falling water and long, long silences. He turned his attention to the trail again, picking his way as carefully as he could.

Get down in the trees, at least. Hide.

A shiver trembled over him uncontrollably. He had *seen* that face, there was no question about that. He hadn't been dreaming, and he wasn't crazy. He didn't bother pinching himself; he was sore enough without that.

He kept moving as fast as he dared. He had to cross the

21

stream, and it was high and turbulent. The icy water soaked him up to his hips. His tennis shoes squished on the rocks.

Get hold of yourself, boy.

He picked up a sharp rock and kept it in his hand. What had that thing *been?* He wasn't superstitious, at least ordinarily, and he had seen enough corpses to be assured that they didn't do much strolling around. Okay. The thing looked like a man, so it must *be* a man. But what was it—he still couldn't think of it as he—doing there? Another fisherman? Surely he would have seen him, or heard him. A hermit? Ridiculous—he couldn't survive long in this country, not without a house and wood for a fire.

Wes began to get mad. He had left a basket full of golden trout up there, to say nothing of his rod and his hat. But he wasn't about to turn around and go back. The man had been big, perhaps a lunatic of some kind. Get some help, maybe, and then go up there in the daylight and see what was going on . . .

He heard a noise to his right.

The stream?

Some animal?

He increased his pace, holding the rock tightly in his hand. It was faster going down than coming up. He should reach the timber line in a minute or two. Should he keep going, try for the car? He was warming up now, feeling a little better, but it would be cold when he stopped, and more than three hours until sunrise.

He decided on the car.

He settled into a steady, loose-jointed walk, almost a trot. His feet squished and slipped, but he kept his balance. Time was healing the shock a little now.

Must be some natural explanation. An airplane crash? Maybe I should have said something, tried to help . . .

But he kept moving.

Trees began to loom up around him, and he caught the lush smell of wet pines. The moonlight was filtered now, and

22

shadows tricked him on the path. He forded the stream again, kept going.

The path twisted sharply to the right.

Wes took the curve almost at a run, then stopped as though he had slammed full-tilt into a brick wall.

The same man was waiting for him on the trail.

He stood there, not moving, only half revealed by the chilled radiance of the moonlight. His face was as dead white as it had seemed in the cave. He was tall, taller than Wes, and thin. His eyes were living shadows in the pallor of his face.

"Who are you?" Wes called. His voice was higher than he had intended. "What do you want?"

The man said nothing. The brook gurgled in the night.

"Talk, damn you! What the hell're you trying to pull?"

No answer.

Wes steadied himself, gripped the rock in his hand. He was *not* going to run back up the mountain again. "Get out of my way," he said.

The man—if such he was—did not move.

Wes had been a reasonably creditable halfback in his high school days, and he had run over bigger men than this. He took his glasses off, put them in his trouser pocket, where they wouldn't be hit directly. Then he squinted, took a deep breath, and rushed the man standing in the trail, his rock ready to swing.

Quite calmly the man raised his arm. He had something in his hand. The something gave a soft *choog* and Wes Chase found himself flat on the ground, his face actually touching one of the man's shoes. He had never seen a shoe like it before.

He seemed to be fully conscious, but he could not move. He heard his heart thudding in his chest. He could not feel the ground under him. He was suddenly peaceful, peaceful beyond all reason. It was the peace of a dream, where nothing mattered, for soon you would wake up and it would all go away. . . .

It didn't go away.

23

The man—it *must* be a man—did not speak. He picked Wes up and tossed him onto his shoulder, not ungently, but with a singular lack of concern. *Like a sack of potatoes,* Wes thought.

The man began to climb back up the mountain. *I weigh almost two hundred pounds, he can't possibly lug me all the way to the top.*

But he was doing it. He gasped for breath and set Wes down every few hundred yards while he rested, but he kept going. Wes watched the trees fade out and the rocks begin, and he saw the moon, alone and cold and remote in the night.

Slowly, determinedly, they climbed toward the glacial lake. They turned off toward the rock shelter. Wes saw his trout basket still lying where he had dropped it, and irrelevantly thought that the fish would still be good because it had been so cold. He saw his rod case, too, but his hat, wherever it had fallen, was outside his field of vision.

The man went into the cave first and pulled Wes in after him. Then he dragged him some fifteen feet across the cave floor, to where Wes had first seen the metallic reflection he had thought was a vein of ore.

Not ore. Door.

The man opened a concealed port that looked like the hatch of a submarine. Pale radiance, not unlike the moonlight outside, spilled into the cavern. The man went through the port and pulled Wes after him.

Then he shut the port. Wes heard the distinct click as it locked.

The man dragged him into a semblance of a sitting position against one wall and then backed off. Wes tried to move, but failed. He had no sensation of pressure where he sat or where he leaned against the wall. He was dead from the neck down.

But his eyes worked. He looked around as best he could.

He was in a large rock vault, perhaps forty yards across at its deepest point. It was apparently a natural cave of some sort,

24

although it had been cleared of all debris until it was rather featureless.

And, of course, it had been sealed off from the world by that curious entry port.

It was utterly silent except for the sound of breathing—his own and the man's.

The vault was not empty. That was the worst part. Wes knew that his normal reactions had been somehow inhibited, but he felt a tendril of apprehension at what he saw in the far wall.

There were niches cut into the rock.

Five of them.

The light was not good in the chamber, coming as it did from tubes like flashlights, but he could see that there were bodies in four of the slots. The fifth one was empty, but it was no great feat of mental gymnastics to figure out who had been there before.

Forget about an airplane crash, then.

Forget about hermits.

Forget about fishermen.

The man looked at him, his white face expressionless. He glanced at the figures in the niches, as though checking.

Then the man moved toward Wes, his eyes very bright, and stretched out his hands.

chapter 3

WES CHASE COULD NOT MOVE.

The moment was intolerable, and it would not end. The cave, the niches, the hands—all were razor-sharp in his mind. He had seen many men die, and had often wondered, rather casually, how death would come to him. His life did not flash through his brain. Instead, a moment out of time was pinpointed and a line he had read in college shouted at him, insanely, over and over:

This is the way the world ends, this is the way the world ends, this is the way——

But it wasn't.

Incredibly, the man's hands touched him and were gentle; there was no malice in them. Wes looked into the man's eyes. They were a clear gray, and he could read nothing in them. The face was a human face—there was a human skull under that flesh. Wes ticked them off: mandible, maxilla, zygomatic arch, nasal cavity, orbits, frontal bone . . .

26

And yet the face was a face unlike any other he had ever seen. It was pasty in its skin texture, but that wasn't the important thing. The proportions were odd in a way he could not define. And the *expression*. Eyes bright, skin taut, thin lips open, breathing fast——

Hate?

Hunger?

Hope?

The hands went over him lightly. His pockets were emptied. His watch was taken from his wrist. The gold wedding ring on his finger was examined, then left where it was. The man was looking for something, Wes was certain of that. But what?

The loot was something less than sensational. A brown billfold Jo had given him for Christmas a year ago. Some loose change—a quarter, two nickels, four pennies. A black comb, not too clean and with one tooth missing; Wes had been meaning to get a new one at the drugstore. A key ring with three keys on it. One was for his car, one for his home on Beverly Glen off Sunset, and one for his Westwood office. Two packs of cigarettes, one of them crumpled and almost empty. A folder of paper matches, also pretty well shot. Two chocolate bars wrapped in shiny paper. A couple of trout flies and a stray, faded salmon egg. No handkerchief—Wes remembered that he had used that for a pillow; it was probably still over there on the rocks.

The man sat down on the cave floor and examined the things intently. Intently? It was more than that. He studied them with an eagerness that bordered on desperation.

The watch seemed to interest him the most. He held it to his ear and listened to it tick. He fiddled with it uncertainly, then wound it a little and moved the hands. He shook his head as though he were disappointed.

It's a good watch. What's wrong with it?

The man turned his attention to the billfold next. He took four dollar bills out of it and studied them. He rubbed them with his fingers. He hesitated, then placed the bills in a pile with the coins. He rifled the rest of the billfold carefully, frowning at the assortment of cards, licenses, and the like. There was one photograph, in color, of Jo. Wes remembered the picture well —it had been taken three years ago, on her birthday. Jo had been wearing a tweed skirt and a brown cashmere sweater; she looked fresh and clean and young. A pang of regret stabbed through Wes, cutting through the haze of the drug. But it passed, he couldn't hold it. Dimly he recognized that it was just as well.

The man took a cigarette out of the pack that was already open, sniffed it, tore the paper off, and looked at the tobacco. He tasted it, frowned, and rubbed it off his tongue with his wrist. He picked up the matches, nodded to himself, and struck one on the first try. He watched it burn down almost to his fingers, then blew it out.

He looked at the keys, tossed them into a pile with the dollar bills and the coins. Then he picked up one of the candy bars and scratched it experimentally with a fingernail. His eyes brightened. With a feverish excitement he ripped the paper off and stared at the brown chocolate with the almond lumps. He hesitated, clearly fighting with himself about something.

The man got up, paced the rock floor, fingering the chocolate bar nervously. Twice he made motions as though he were going to eat it, but each time he hesitated, caught himself, stopped.

He doesn't know whether or not it's edible. Where can he be from if he's never seen a chocolate bar before?

The man came to some decision. He broke off two squares of chocolate, knelt down by Wes, and gently opened the doctor's mouth. Then he crumbled the chocolate between his fingers, threw an almond away, and placed the shredded chocolate on Wes's tongue, a little at a time. Wes started to gag, and was unable to chew. But he could swallow, if he took it easy, and he got the chocolate down.

Guinea pig, he thought. He remembered the little test animals in their cages on the top floor of the hospital. He remembered,

28

too, one of the daughters of old Doc Stuart—Louise, her name had been—and how shocked she was when she found out that the guinea pigs were injected with disease strains to see what would happen. . . .

The chocolate was good, anyway.

The man sat down and made an obvious effort at self-discipline. He sat quietly, watching and waiting. Several hours must have gone by, but it was difficult now for Wes to keep track of the time.

The man got up finally, felt Wes's forehead, looked at his eyes and his tongue. And he smiled. The effect was startling, as though a movie monster had paused momentarily in his dim-witted pursuit of the dim-witted heroine and tossed off a minstrel joke or two.

Then the man ate the chocolate bars.

Ate them?

He *demolished* them, swallowing convulsively, as a man trapped in a desert might hurl himself into a stream, desperate for water.

The man smiled again and rubbed his hands together in a curiously out-of-place gesture of satisfaction. A little color appeared in his pale cheeks. Even his black and rather lank hair seemed to lose some of its lifelessness.

Evidently encouraged by his new-found energy, the man went to work with a will. He put Wes down on the rock floor and carefully undressed him, taking mental note of every button, buckle, and zipper. He covered Wes up with his own clothing, and then struggled to dress himself in his new clothes. He managed it, though not without a few muttered sounds that might very well have been swearing of some sort. Wes was surprised to see that his clothes were not a bad fit at all; apparently the man was not as tall as he looked.

The man stuffed his pockets, paying special attention to the money, and slipped the watch over his wrist. He seemed nervous again, but determined.

He's going to Lake City, Wes thought, and was suddenly warm with hope. *He's done his best, but he still doesn't look like the All-American Boy. Somebody's bound to notice him. Somebody's bound to recognize those clothes. Jo will have called the police by now, they'll be watching . . .*

The man opened the port and went out into the cave. The port clicked shut behind him.

Wes still could not move. He lay on his back, covered by the man's clothing, and out of the corner of his eye he could just see the niches in the far wall, where the four silent bodies slept.

He hoped *they* didn't wake up.

Even through the fog of the drug doubts assailed him. Would the man actually *get* to Lake City? It would be a pretty fair walk if he didn't spot the car. Could he drive? If he had never seen a chocolate bar, had he ever seen an automobile?

Suppose he made it to Lake City. The police would be looking for Wes, not for a man they had never seen. Would they spot his clothes? After all, they were just the standard fisherman's rig. The trousers were torn a little, but there was nothing very unusual about that. And the hat was missing, unless the man picked it up on the way. The car was the best bet, the car with the California plates. If he took it——

How odd would a man have to look before a merchant would call the police? If Wes were running a drugstore and that man came in, what would he think? Probably just write him off as a weirdie and let it go at that. Remember, during the war, the two guys in Nazi uniforms who strolled through Times Square, or wherever it was . . .

Time seemed to be passing rapidly. Wes was not quite asleep, but not completely awake either. It was as though he had a slight fever, dozing in bed, waiting for a cold to go away.

He knew what the man was after in town, or thought he did. He was obviously starving. If Wes had been in that position, he would have tried to buy some food, and it seemed reasonable

30

to suppose that the man would think along the same lines. But there were only four dollars in that billfold. If the man was figuring on stocking up on provisions, he was in for a rude surprise.

Wes felt suddenly cold. It was not so very far from here, back in the old days, where a miner had gotten snowed in for the winter with three companions, without enough food to go around. When spring came, the miner came out of the cabin alone, sleek and well fed. The story was that he had died in the penitentiary, a confirmed vegetarian. . . .

If the man couldn't get enough supplies in town, then what?

Wes tried to turn his thoughts to more pleasant subjects.

That turned out to be not so easy, however. No matter where he started, his thoughts always came back to the man, to say nothing of his four snoozing companions. Who were they? Where could they have come from?

And what did they *want?*

In spite of himself Wes had to admire the man. Looked at through his own eyes, he was doing a brave and remarkable thing—even a fantastic thing. He seemed to be utterly alien, completely unfamiliar with even such a common article as a chocolate bar. He either did not know English or refused to speak it. Presumably Wes looked just as strange to him as he did to Wes. And yet he was willing to put on another man's clothes and try to find his way to a town where he could buy food he had never seen before with money he couldn't possibly understand.

The man was having his troubles too.

Somehow that made Wes feel a little better.

He dozed off, fell into an uneasy sleep.

He was awakened by the click of the port when it opened. The man hurried through and closed the port behind him. He looked utterly exhausted, and he was trembling violently. Wes tried to get up, and still couldn't move.

The man looked at Wes—how? Angrily? Hopelessly? He put

31

down a cardboard box he was carrying and unpacked it. It was pitiful, even to Wes. Four loaves of bread. Two cans of asparagus. And about fifty assorted candy bars.

Looking very pale again, the man stretched out on the rocks next to Wes, sighed a little, and went to sleep. He snored.

There was nothing to look at. Wes felt that by now he had memorized every detail of the vault, from the dark shapes in the niches to the cracks on the rocks that hemmed him in. He was no longer tired, and he thought his mind was somewhat clearer. Oddly, his terror had left him. He was still afraid, still uncertain, but the whole affair had taken on a remote dreamlike quality, in which nothing was played for keeps and everything would somehow be all right in the end.

He recognized the symptoms of shock in himself.

That means the stuff is wearing off. If I can just get hold of myself before he wakes up——

He waited. There was nothing else to do.

He thought of the sleeping man next to him. He had made it to Lake City, evidently. Had he walked or taken the car? He had bought some things, and that must have involved some experimentation with the money. Surely, *surely,* he had created a stir in Lake City. Sooner or later someone would make the connection with Wes, if he hadn't done so already. And then——

Could they find him?

And what would they find? A living man—or something else?

The time passed very slowly. Wes thought he was coming out of it a little, but not fast enough. And when the man at his side woke up, Wes could still do no more than move his head a trifle from side to side.

Here we go again.

The man got up and looked closely at Wes. Wes lay very still, almost holding his breath. The man smiled a little and touched his shoulder in what Wes interpreted as a reassuring gesture.

32

Or is he just picking out a haunch?

The man stretched and ate two candy bars, not with any very obvious relish. Then he walked over to the niches and examined the forms that still slept in them. He watched them for a long time, touched one of them gently.

There was no response.

Wes was glad of it.

He didn't know *what* would come out of that niche, and he was in absolutely no hurry to find out.

The man took out the gun, the same one he had used on Wes. He checked it carefully, reset a dial on the butt end of it.

He licked his lips.

Wes suddenly got very cold, but recovered himself promptly. *Stop thinking about it! You're making it worse!*

In a somewhat more objective frame of mind Wes realized what the man was going to do. It was obvious enough. No matter how alien the man looked, his thought processes were not by any means impossible to follow. If he couldn't buy enough food for a decent meal, he had to get it some other way.

Therefore he was going hunting.

The man went out again through the portal, taking his gun with him.

Wes was decidedly curious despite his position. If the man were just after food, and if he could really use that gun for hunting, why go all the way to Lake City in the first place? There was plenty of game in these mountains, especially if you weren't overly particular what you were eating. Wouldn't it have been simpler just to bag a deer or something right off the bat?

But I don't think he knew how far away Lake City was. And maybe he was after something more important than food.

What?

Information, of course.

He's trying to find out something about us. I'm positive he's never seen a man like me before. He's looking for something.

What? And why?

The man was gone a long time. When he came back he had fresh meat with him, already skinned and cleaned. It looked like a wolf. He had also carried back some dead wood and twigs, so he must have been down below timber line.

He built a fire very carefully, using bark for paper. He lit it with one of the matches he had taken from Wes, and it caught at once. It was just a small blaze, but Wes could feel its warmth. He noticed that the smoke was carried out through the top of the vault; there must be an air duct of some sort up there.

The man sliced off four steaks with a knife Wes had not seen before, and began to roast them on the end of sticks. Juices dropped into the fire and sizzled.

Wes could smell the meat cooking. His mouth literally watered, and he was suddenly desperately hungry.

When the steaks were done, the man went to work on one. There was nothing now of the gulping haste he had shown with the first candy bars. He took his time, chewing each piece thoroughly, savoring every bit of it. The pallor in his face was much less marked now than when Wes had first seen him.

He got up and took the metallic gun from the pocket of the jacket he had borrowed from Wes. Once more he reset the dial on the butt.

He aimed it at Wes's shoulder.

The gun made a whispered *choog*.

Wes tried to brace himself, but felt nothing.

The man waited.

And then, slowly, incredibly, feeling flowed back into Wes's body. It felt like ice water. His skin prickled and itched. He tried to move his arm, and the effort was agony, as though his arm had been asleep and he had suddenly smacked it against a door.

He began to shake violently.

He was coming out of it.

The man watched, and waited, and said nothing at all.

chapter 4

IT WAS LIKE BEING BORN AGAIN.

Weston Chase could feel the life coming back to him, and life was a million icy needles in his veins. Sometimes it was better to be only half alive. When you were sick enough you didn't feel the pain. When you got well enough to hurt and to remember, things got tough.

He lay on the cave floor and wanted to scream. Perhaps he did; he couldn't be sure. He was sick and miserable and empty. His mouth tasted like stale tobacco smoke. His skull ached as though there were a knife in it. His body was so sore he couldn't even crawl.

But that was only physical.

He could take that.

But the *other* things——

He was in a cave with a maniac, or worse. And Jo didn't

know where he was, *nobody* knew where he was. How long had he been here? What was Jo thinking? Surely she would know he hadn't just run out on her—or would she?

Images blinked on and off like slides in his brain. Jo with her swimming pool he had been so sarcastic about. The kid next door who had fallen off his bicycle, the blood on his head, and Jo helping him fix the boy up. A nice boy, the son he had always wanted. And Jo that night in her house, the year before they were married——

Jo.

He groaned, he wanted to cry like a baby. God, this was fantastic, a nightmare, it couldn't happen——

A pale hand slipped under him.

He was pulled into a sitting position. The white, strange face was next to his.

Dracula, Wes thought hysterically. *I'm in a damn silly vampire movie. Garlic! Where's the garlic?*

He laughed. When he heard himself he stopped.

The pale man hooked something over Wes's ears. Glasses. His glasses. Then he opened Wes's mouth and put something in it. Wes choked, started to chew. His jaws didn't work properly, but rich juices trickled down his throat, warming him. Meat. Tough, but sweet and clean.

The man fed him, and Wes ate. He swallowed one steak and half of another before he was through, telling himself he should take it easy but being too hungry to care. Then the man gave him some cold water from a skin bag.

"Thanks," Wes said. His voice was a croak.

The man nodded, but said nothing. He went back to work on his own meal, chewing slowly and thoughtfully, as though making up for lost time. Wes lay on the floor, feeling a drowsy strength flow back into him. Now was his chance, he thought. Get up, slug that man, get out somehow——

Before he could frame much of a plan he was asleep. He did

36

not dream. He had no way of telling how long he slept, but he awoke refreshed. He opened one eye.

The man was watching him, smiling a little. The man took his arm, helped him up. Wes was dizzy, but he could stand. The man took him step by step over to the circular port that was the only exit to the vault. He stood him against it, then backed off and sat down on the floor.

Free. I'm free. He's letting me go.

Desperately Wes fumbled at the projections on the port. He pulled them, pushed them, twisted them, hit at them with his fists. Nothing happened. He put his shoulder against the port and pushed. The circular door did not move. He backed off, ran at it blindly.

It was, literally, like running into a stone wall.

He collapsed, sobbing.

The man picked him up, gave him another drink of water. Then he looked at Wes and shook his head. The meaning was clear enough. Wes couldn't get out unless the man let him out.

And Wes suspected it would be a sub-arctic afternoon in hell before *that* happened.

The man sat down and gave Wes a cold piece of steak. Wes ate it without thinking. His mind was a perfect blank, holding the terror out.

Then the man leaned forward. He pointed at himself. "Arvon," he said slowly and distinctly. His voice was low and calm.

Wes hesitated. Then he nodded, pointed at himself. "Wes," he said. "Wes Chase."

The man smiled eagerly.

In a way that was the real beginning.

Wes Chase didn't know a phoneme from a hole in the ground, and if he had ever heard of a lexicon he would have vaguely associated it with a Roman lawgiver. Linguistics hadn't exactly been all the rage of the campus when Wes was taking

37

pre-med at Ohio State, and the medical school at the University of Cincinnati had emphasized practical subjects.

Of course, a man never knew what was going to be practical and what wasn't. This wasn't the first time that Wes had regretted the pressures of a busy life, a life that nibbled you to death with schedules and telephones and appointments and runny noses. If only there were time to find out a few things, to read, to listen . . .

But it was a little late now.

Wes *did* know, from his agonizing battle with Latin and the damnable tripartite division of Gaul, that learning a language was apt to be a losing proposition even under the best of circumstances. When a man had to learn a language from scratch, without the medium of a common language to explain things in, it should take a spell.

It did.

Nevertheless, Arvon learned with incredible rapidity. He made no attempt to teach Wes his own language, whatever *that* might have been, but concentrated on mastering English. He started with nouns, things that could be pointed to: cave, shirt, shoes, meat, candy. He kept a list of words, writing them down on a curious sort of tablet, and Wes soon caught on to the fact that Arvon was not so much after the words themselves as he was interested in the significant sounds that went into them. He used recording symbols Wes had never seen before, but he assumed that they were phonetic marks of some type. He started with hundreds, marking every tone and pause and inflection, but rapidly whittled his alphabet down to a realistic series of marks as he discovered what counted in English and what didn't. Then he went on to the structure of the language, the way the word units were strung together. When he got the hang of the agent-verb-object series, his progress was rapid.

Still, it took time.

There was time to be bored, even in this uncanny, impossible vault in the rock of a Colorado mountain. There was time to eat fresh meat and fish until he was sick of them. There was time to be impatient, and worry, and be afraid.

There was too much time to remember the life he had cherished so little—the life that waited for him now at the foot of a winding trail, where an icy trout stream chuckled out into a valley of green and gold. A valley in the sun. He had not seen the sun for—how long?

He could see every detail of his life in the sun: the clear warmth of morning before the smog rolled in, the carbon trails down the Hollywood Freeway, the dark sparkling green of dichondra under the sprinklers, the damp red banks of geraniums, the bright flowered shirts by the sea in Santa Monica. . . .

He could see it.

And Jo—where was Jo? Was she lonely in that empty house that they had shared? Or was she—the thought would not go away—was she just a little glad that he was gone? She had failed him in many ways, but what kind of a life had *he* given her, really?

There was time for too many memories, not all of them pleasant.

But Arvon stuck with it, with a steady patience that still could not hide the light in his eyes. He cracked the language barrier, imperfectly at first, and then the vault was a little less lonely, a little less alien.

Wes was caught in a situation he could not control; he recognized that and tried to adjust himself to it. He was as nearly helpless as a man could be, but some of his fear was gone now.

He even managed to forget the bodies in the niches, at least most of the time.

He began to feel a charge of excitement, a thrill of being close to something utterly beyond his understanding. It was a sensation he had had once before in his life, when he had started out to do endocrine research soon after leaving medical school.

He had given that up little by little; he had never really known why.

Well, he couldn't give *this* up.

Almost, he was glad that he couldn't.

He made himself as comfortable as he could, and he knew that he was sitting on a story that would make the first atomic bomb seem like a back-page gossip item for a movie columnist. It was not an altogether unpleasant sensation.

He talked, and listened, and tried to do the hardest thing of all.

He tried to understand.

Wes had developed, over the years, a rule-of-thumb psychology that all doctors had to have. Medicine was not all midnight jaunts with the accelerator floored and crises in the operating room, particularly if you happened to be an eye, ear, nose, and throat man. A great deal of his practice was routine, and a lot of it was a crashing bore. He played a game with himself during the long office afternoons, trying to size up new patients as Miss Hill showed them through the door. Were they really sick, or after drugs on one pretext or another? Were they the nervous type who caught pneumonia every time they sneezed, or were they actually in bad shape? What did they do for a living? More importantly, sometimes, what did they *want* to do for a living?

Wes was pretty good at it. He could often peg a person within two minutes, and be close enough to be of some aid in the diagnosis. But how did you evaluate the personality of a man with whom you had *nothing* in common? How much of what he thought of as personality was just a cut of clothes, a way of speaking, a choice of familiar pastimes, a taste for Toynbee or funny books?

He was no fool. There was nothing to be gained by panic and hysteria, but the plain fact was that Arvon was a man utterly outside the frame of his experience. Wherever he had come from, whatever he was, he was *different*. How could you tell what his motives were? They might be anything. How could you tell whether he meant you harm or was just defending himself? Defending—against what threat? How could you tell whether he told you the truth or lies? How could you tell what he wanted information *for?*

And yet Wes felt a sort of trust, almost a kinship. If it hadn't been for Jo and the discomfort——

"Look," Arvon said. "Paintings."

He handed Wes a packet of colored prints.

"Photographs," Wes corrected him.

He stared at them. Many were of rolling plains, knee-deep in grasses. Some were of snow and ice. Several showed strange men in skins. They looked a little like Eskimos. Wes tried to recall the Disney short on Eskimos, but couldn't remember the details. In any event, they weren't *quite* Eskimos, he was certain of that. There were shots of animals he had never seen —a great shaggy beast like an elephant, a thing like an overgrown buffalo.

Mostly there were fields, and grasses, and ice.

"Your—ummm—world?" Wes asked, feeling a little foolish.

Arvon looked blank.

Wes borrowed the man's tablet and the writing instrument. *Let's see now,* he thought. *How do they do it in the movies?*

He started with the sun, drawing a circle in the center of the page. So far, so good. But what came between the sun and the Earth? Wes had never had time to bother with a course in astronomy, and he was neither more nor less ignorant of such matters than the bulk of his fellow citizens.

Well, eliminate some of the outer planets. Pluto, that was the little one way out on the edge; throw that one away. But what else? How many planets were there, anyhow? Eight? Nine? Ten? He shook his head. Mars was the one he was after; that was where aliens always came from in the movies, so there must be *some* reason behind the choice. But which side

41

of the Earth was Mars on? Toward the sun or in the direction of Pluto?

"Hell," he said.

He drew ten planets in a straight line out from the sun and handed the tablet to Arvon. Arvon looked at it with blank incomprehension. After all, it was just a series of circles on a piece of paper. Arvon studied it solemnly, and finally folded it up and put it in his pocket.

So much for *that*.

Time passes slowly in a confined space. Wes got his watch back so he could keep track of the hours, but he still had no idea how long he had been in the vault before he was able to read the dial on his watch again. Quite possibly it was autumn outside, with winter on the way. It would be cold in the mountains, and snow would make the trail a tough one, if he ever saw it again.

It took him two days of concentrated effort to get across to Arvon the idea that he wanted to write Jo a letter—just a note saying that he was okay, that he loved her, that he would explain everything to her someday. He even wrote such a letter, explained about addresses, and spent a miserable few hours trying to get across the concept of stamps.

Arvon took the note and read it. He read it not once, but many times. He took it apart and put it back together again. And then he shook his head sadly.

"But why? It can't hurt you—can't *hurt* you. Small thing to ask——"

Arvon refused firmly. "Desire to help," he said slowly. "Desire to help, but must *not* help." He groped for words. "Risk. Danger. Big chance."

Wes felt his unnatural calmness desert him. "But you have no right to keep me here like this! You have explained nothing, done nothing, said nothing. What the devil kind of a man are you?"

Arvon frowned, puzzled.

42

Oh God, this is impossible!

Then, unexpectedly, Arvon tried to answer him. *"Right,"* he said. "Hard word. Very hard word. Right for you or right for me?"

"Both," Wes almost shouted. "Right's right."

Arvon smiled and shook his head. "I try to explain," he said. He stopped, unsatisfied. "I *will* try to explain," he corrected himself. "You try to understand. I—we—mean no harm to you. I—we—do what we must. *Understand.*"

Wes waited.

The man's strange gray eyes grew distant, lost. His tongue groped with words that were not his words. He tried to tell a story that was beyond telling, across a gulf that could not be bridged.

And Weston Chase sat in the bare rock vault, where a tiny fire threw ghostly shadows across the dark forms who slept as only the dead may sleep, and the still air was hushed with long, long silences. He sat, and he listened, and he tried to understand.

The man talked on and on and on, and the fire grew low, and the pale radiance in the cavern was like the frozen silver of the moon. . . .

chapter 5

THE SHIP WAS ALONE.

She was moving, and moving fast, but there was nothing around her to show her speed. She seemed suspended in a featureless universe of gray, transfixed in an empty fog, beyond space, beyond time, beyond understanding.

There were no stars, no planets, no far galaxies like milky jewels against the shadowed velvet of space.

There was the ship, and the grayness, and that was all.

Inside the ship a plump, balding man named Nlesine jerked a stubby thumb toward the blue metal wall that sealed them from the desolation Outside. "In my humble opinion," he said, "that is the ideal home for humanity out there. We got off on the wrong foot right at the start, as any idiot should be able to see—even you, Tsriga. Man is slime, an infection in the cosmos. Why should he live on green planets under blue skies? If ever there were an organism that had earned an isolated place in Nowhere, man is it."

The high, irritating hum of the atomics powering the distortion field filled the ship. The sensation was precisely that of listening to a bomb falling toward you, a bomb that never hit.

Tsriga, his rather flashy clothes startling in the subdued green room, was bitingly conscious of his youth, but determined to cover it up at all costs. He knew that Nlesine was baiting him; very well, he would go him one better. "You've understated the case," he said. "You're too optimistic, as usual. I think that even Nowhere is too fine a place for us. What we need is Somewhere more gruesome than Nowhere."

Nlesine laughed. He laughed considerably more than the joke warranted. He laughed until the tears ran out of his eyes. "You're a card, Tsriga," he said. "You should insure that priceless sense of humor for a billion credits, so that you may always be a little ray of sunshine in our lives."

"Go to hell," Tsriga said, and moved away.

Nlesine stopped laughing and turned to Arvon, who was seated across from him reading a novel. "What do you think, handsome?"

Arvon lowered the book reluctantly. "I think you ride the kid too much."

Nlesine made an impolite noise. "He's got to grow up sometime."

"Don't we all?"

Nlesine snorted. "A great line. Sounds like one of my own novels. You read too many books, Arvon. You're turning into an Intellectual. You should get out on the farm, sniff the barnyard smells, learn to *live*."

Arvon smiled a little, his tall body relaxed in his chair, his book balanced easily in his strong hand. His gray eyes were more puzzled than amused, however. "I've never understood why you work so hard to be the Great Cynic, Nlesine."

"Meaning that I'm obnoxious enough without trying?"

45

"Meaning that it must get a bit tiresome, even for you."

"Why don't you preach to me about Golden Humanity, like Kolraq does? Explain about the unity of life, the harmony of the spheres, the cuddly qualities of the little furry creatures ——"

"No, thanks," Arvon said, raising his book like a shield. "I'd rather read."

The ship shuddered slightly; the high hum increased its pitch to an uncomfortable whine.

A door slid open and Hafij, the navigator, stepped into the cabin. He was erect and calm, his strange black eyes sweeping the others with something that was more unconcern than contempt. "We're going to come out of it in a minute," he said. "Better strap yourselves in."

"The field still acting up?" Arvon asked.

"Some, yes."

"There won't be any—trouble—will there?" Tsriga wiped his hands on an overly fancy handkerchief.

The navigator shrugged.

Nlesine rose to the occasion. "It looks bad to Nlesine," he muttered, employing his favorite phrase. "We'll have to sleep our way home, if we ever come out of the distortion field at all. Is the emergency stuff all set up, Hafij?"

"It's ready," Hafij said, and didn't laugh.

"Hold on," Nlesine said, sitting up straighter. "You mean there's really going to be——"

"Better strap yourselves in," the navigator said, and went back to the control room.

The three men stared at each other, suddenly closer than they had been in the four years they had been together.

"It looks bad to Nlesine," Nlesine said wryly.

"It even looks bad to Arvon," Arvon muttered.

Tsriga, very young and very afraid, strapped himself in his chair and closed his eyes.

The ship shuddered again. Somewhere in the walls a cable began to spark hissingly.

The gray emptiness around them seemed very near, pressing in on them, suffocating them——

"Here goes nothing," Arvon said.

The lights dimmed.

They waited.

The ship came out of it.

When it happened, it happened all at once. There was no transition. The ship blinked out of nothingness, back into normal space, back into a dark sea where the stars were gleaming islands and no winds ever blew. It was a friendlier place, somehow, than what they had left behind them. Vast it was, this ocean where worlds were dust, and yet it was familiar, too, for it was the universe that had given birth to man; it could be understood, however dimly.

The ship swam through the deeps at close to the speed of light, but there was no sensation of movement, and the stars maintained their chill remoteness.

The ship still had a long way to go.

"Looks like we made it," Arvon said, unstrapping himself.

"We haven't landed yet," Nlesine reminded him.

"That *was* a rough pull-out," Tsriga said, the color coming back into his cheeks. "Nobody can tell me we weren't in trouble that time."

The sound of the atomics dwindled to a steady, throbbing hum—smooth, comforting, precise.

The control room door slid open again and Hafij stuck his head in. "Derryoc in here?" asked the navigator.

"Yeah," said Nlesine. "He's hiding under my chair."

"Probably back in the library," Arvon said. "You want him?"

"We should touch down in another twelve hours. Seyehi wants to get the computers set up for the first scan, and he says he doesn't want to have to do it all over again when Derryoc quits pounding his ear long enough to think up objections."

"I'll get him," Arvon said.

He got up and went back along the main corridor to the library. As he had expected, Derryoc was there, seated at a long table, squinting into a viewer. The anthropologist had films scattered all over the place, and had managed to accumulate a fair-sized collection of empty glasses, a few of which still had liquor in them.

Probably, Arvon thought, the man hadn't even noticed the rough passage when they had pulled out of the distortion field. Not because he was drunk, of course—Arvon had never seen Derryoc drunk despite the amount of drink he stowed away. But when he got immersed in one of his problems, the rest of the world might as well not exist. It was a habit of mind that Arvon recognized but found impossible to understand.

"Derryoc," he said.

The anthropologist waved a hand irritably. "Minute," he said.

Arvon gave him his minute, then tried again. "We're landing in twelve hours. Seyehi wants to get set up for a scan."

The anthropologist looked up. There were dark circles under his eyes, and his hair hadn't been combed in a week. He was a big man, running a little to fat, but he had an air of competence about him. Arvon had always rather liked Derryoc, but the anthropologist kept his distance. Derryoc tended to feel that anyone who wasn't a scientist of some sort really wasn't worth fooling with; Arvon knew he was just a playboy to him despite the zoology he had learned to qualify for the trip.

"Twelve hours?"

"Yes. We're out in normal space again."

"I wondered what was wrong with the damn lights." He pushed the viewer back, stood up, and stretched.

"Think we'll find anything this time?" Arvon asked.

The anthropologist looked at him. "No. Do you?"

Arvon shook his head. "No, but I hope we do."

"Hope's tricky. Don't rely on it. You know how many planets we've checked, counting all the ships that have ever gone out?"

"Around a thousand, I'd guess."

"One thousand two hundred and one, counting *our* last stop. So the odds are one thousand two hundred and one to one that we'll find what we always find."

"Statistics can be misleading."

"Not like hopes, Arvon. Always bet with the odds and you come out ahead."

"Mind if I come along to the control room with you?"

"Not at all." Derryoc smiled. "What's the matter—Nlesine wearing your hopes down?"

"Something like that," Arvon admitted.

The two men walked out of the library, into the corridor. They walked slowly toward the control room, and as they walked the ship around them floated through the great night, toward a new sun and new worlds—and, perhaps, a new answer to the problem that faced them all, the problem that had to be solved.

Inside the control room the atmosphere of the ship was subtly different. It was not a physical change; no gauge or meter could have registered the tension in that air. It was a question of personality. It was there, and you responded to it, but it was not easy to pin down.

Partly it was the room itself. At sea the man at the wheel is the man who feels the waves and the currents and the dark depths below, and it is not otherwise with the ships that sail that mightier sea of space.

Partly it was Hafij. The navigator was a man at home in space as other men never were; his thin body and his black eyes, remote as the stars themselves, *belonged* in this room, and were a part of it. It would not be true to say that he loved the dark recesses between the worlds, but he was drawn to them as a man is drawn to his woman, and to them he always returned.

Partly it was Seyehi: not much to look at, unobtrusive, he blended with the equipment in the room. More precisely, he was an extension of the computers he ran. The others called him Feedback, and he always smiled at the name, as though it were a compliment. He knew his machines, and he lived with them, and it might have been true to say that he loved them.

But mostly it was Wyik.

Wyik was the Captain to all of them; it was impossible to think of him as anything else. He must have had a life before he went into space, before he began the search that he pursued with a granite hardness that none of the others could match. He must have been born, been raised in a family, lived, laughed, loved. He must have had such a life, but none of them had ever seen it. This was his fourth trip, and twenty years in space is a long time for any man. The Captain was short, wiry, tough. He rarely smiled, not even when he got drunk, which was seldom. He was ablaze with energy. Even standing still, eyes staring into the plates, he seemed charged with electricity, tense, ready for sudden movement.

The control room was different. In the rest of the ship men might joke about the thing that had taken them light-years from their home, the thing that mocked them on every world they visited. In the rest of the ship men might relax, and even forget, for a while.

You didn't relax here, and you didn't forget.

Arvon kept out of the way. He was a stranger here; this was not his part of the ship, no matter how much he might have wished it to be.

"Get on with it, Derryoc," the Captain said. His voice was controlled, but vibrantly alive. "We'll be in position for you within eleven hours."

Derryoc looked at Seyehi. "The usual approach?"

The computer man nodded. "We'll make a circuit around the most favorable planet, five miles up. We're set up to scan for everything we can detect at that height: population concentrations, radio waves, energy emissions of any sort at all. We'll make one circuit at the equator first, then cross over the poles. I've got the computers set to make a level analysis of anything we pick up."

"I'll want maps," the anthropologist said.

"You'll have them. Anything else?"

The anthropologist clasped his hands behind his back. "Well, after your computers report that the planet is uninhabited by any so-called intelligent life——"

"You mean *if*, not *after*, Derryoc," the Captain interrupted.

Derryoc shrugged. *"If*, then," he corrected without conviction. "If the inevitable happens, I want Hafij to take her down as close as he can, where I can see for myself. There's always a mathematical chance for a low-energy culture, and I'll want to look at it before we go barging in on it."

"That all?"

"That's all for now." Derryoc turned to the Captain. "You'll have the screens up, Wyik?"

"I won't be taking any chances."

"Right. Come on, Arvon—let's have a drink before we go to work."

They left the control room and went back to the bar, which was little more than a cubicle set into the wall. Derryoc broke out a bottle and two glasses, and the two men drank.

Arvon felt the liquor warming him, and he was glad to have it. He tried not to anticipate the despair that was coming, but the hopelessness piled up with the years—it was not difficult to understand Nlesine's dark outlook, no matter how trying it became.

If only all the planets *were* uninhabited by men.

That wouldn't have been so bad.

"Why did you come out here, anyway?" Derryoc asked suddenly, pouring his second drink. "Didn't you have a deal at home?"

Arvon smiled, remembering. The big home in the country,

51

the tapestries, the books, the warmth. And the cities, the plays, the women. . . .

"I had too much of a deal," he said.

Derryoc downed half the drink at a gulp. "I don't understand you," he said honestly.

"That makes us even," said Arvon.

"We'll never find it, you know," the anthropologist said.

"We've got to find it," Arvon replied. "That's all there is to it."

"More hoping, Arvon?"

"A man can do worse."

The ship plunged on. Framed by stars, she lanced through darkness unimaginable, toward light.

Toward a yellow sun, flanked by two other suns, one near, one far away.

The system of Alpha Centauri, over four light-years from a world called Earth.

chapter 6

KOLRAQ SAT ALONE, HIS THOUGHTS MAKING THE SILENT journey down to the world below the ship. He did not like to be alone at a time like this, but Hafij was occupied, and the navigator was the only man aboard with whom he felt completely at ease.

Something about the stars, he had often thought of Hafij. *He has looked long at the stars, and that is the beginning of wisdom.*

Well, he could not share his thoughts with Hafij now.

Kolraq reflected, not for the first time, that a spaceship was a strange place for a priest. Most of the others, when they thought about him at all, dismissed him as a mystic and let it go at that. It was not a term of condemnation with them; when they stuck the mystic label on him they simply proved to their own satisfaction that he was no part of their world—he became

53

a man to be treated with courtesy, but not a man to take very seriously.

Well, it was an odd business, this being a priest in this day and age. There had been a time on Lortas when the Church had been powerful, but the last century had seen it divided and weak; it was hardly more than a philosophy at best in these days, and at worst——

If only man had never gone into space! If only he had never found what he did find! But no, that was spineless thinking. Surely, a true God was not destroyed by the truth, no matter where it was found. There must be an answer, some other answer than the one men had been finding over and over again, the answer that mocked them on every habitable world in all the abyss of space. . . .

Centaurus Four, now!

There was a chance, there was always a chance. If there was a unity to all life, as he had been taught, as he tried to believe with his heart and soul, then there had to be another answer than the one men had found.

Had to be, *had* to be!

"Ah, Kolraq!" a voice cut in on his thoughts. "What's new in the crystal ball department?"

Lajor, of course. Why couldn't the newsman leave him alone at a time like this? Would the man chatter on the brink of eternity itself? *But these are not charitable thoughts, Kolraq. If you cannot find charity in yourself, why expect it in others?*

"The crystal ball is cloudy, I'm afraid."

Lajor seated himself. He was a sloppy man, sloppy in his dress, in his work, perhaps in his thoughts. True, thought Kolraq, his travel books were more popular than the novels of Nlesine, but they would be sooner forgotten. *Charity, charity!*

Lajor scribbled on a pad. "Centaurus Four, open the door!" He chuckled, and Kolraq dredged up a faint smile. "Big scoop coming up, you know it! We'll go flipping around the old rock pile, with Seyehi's computers buzzing and clacking, and then we'll zoom down and let Derryoc squint at his eternal problems. Then down goes the *Good Hope,* splat! We all get out and scrabble around, and what do I get out of it? Another little old chapter, same as all the rest. Centaurus Four, you're a bore!"

"There's a chance," the priest said. *Was there, was there?*

"Sure, sure." Lajor screwed up his face into a fair imitation of Nlesine's plump features. "But it looks bad to Nlesine!"

"Nlesine has been wrong before," Kolraq said patiently.

"You bet he has, you just bet he has. Why, I remember the time—back before we left old Lortas and set sail into the old sunrise—Nlesine was sounding off about . . ."

Kolraq shut his ears with an effort; the voice at his side became a drone, an irritant, nothing more. *Lord, Lord, are we no better than the rest? Must we bicker and pick at each other, even here, even now, in the Shadow?*

Far below the ship the brown world that was the fourth planet of Alpha Centauri spun through space, orbited around her flaming primary.

In the control room of the *Good Hope,* Derryoc looked up from the computer tapes and shook his head.

"Take her down," he said to the Captain.

Already the ship had eased down out of the endless night of space through a high, thin blue. She had settled through a rolling sea of white clouds, flashed into sunshine and winds and horizons.

Now she went down to where snow-tipped mountains almost ripped her belly. She roared and thundered, this gleaming titan; she ripped through winds and rains, and the air rushed in behind her with a thunder of its own.

She blasted over continents, across tossing seas. She threw her snake shadow over lonely islands and sent birds rising fearfully from forest trees. She flashed across yellow desert sands and left new dunes in her wake.

Derryoc stayed at his viewer-scope, not moving save to make rapid notes on a pad.

After six hours he stood up wearily. "It is the same," he said to Wyik.

The Captain stood steadily. There was no change of expression on his face. His muscles tensed a little more, and that was all. "Would you care to suggest a likely spot for the field investigation?"

The anthropologist consulted his pad. He nodded, gave Hafij the co-ordinates of the best site he had seen.

There was despair in the control room now, an old despair, unvoiced and unheeded. *The same, the same. It was always the same.*

The ship thundered back to the position Derryoc had given. She stood on her tail and rode a boiling column of flame out of the sky, down to the desert sands that waited for her with an ageless patience.

She landed, settled, stopped.

There was silence.

The air was tested, found unbreathable. Since the copter was such a nuisance to assemble, they decided to walk to the site— it was very close anyway. Derryoc, Tsriga, Nlesine, Lajor, and Arvon put on face masks. The others stayed with the ship.

The great airlock port sealed behind them. The outer door hissed open. Derryoc went out first, and down the ladder. Arvon was right behind him.

Arvon shivered, although it was not cold. His boots sunk into the yellow sand, and he stood a moment, listening. The sounds he heard were strange after the mechanical hums of the ship.

The sounds of wind, sighing across the desert, wind that had known ocean seas, and would know them again. The sounds of sand, rustling, sliding, shifting.

The sound was the sound of rain, but the sky above them was a cloudless blue, the visible sun warm and peaceful. Their shadows moved before them, sharply etched on the rippled sand.

Yes, and the sounds were the sounds of death, the dry whispers that spoke of life that had once been, and was no more.

Death, thought Arvon. *Hello, old friend.* . . .

"Come on," called Derryoc, crunching across the desert floor. "Come on, we don't want to get caught out by nightfall."

Arvon fell into line, and single file they made their way across the sand, feeling it trickle into their boots, drift inside their shirts.

A bath will feel good tonight, Arvon thought, and smiled at the utter irrelevance of the notion.

Behind them the ship towered in a land of desolation.

Ahead of them, naked and gaping in the driven sand, waited the thing that had once been a city, the thing that men had once called home.

How do you describe the sadness of centuries? What epitaph do you inscribe on the tombstone of man?

Arvon looked at Nlesine and at Lajor. What lines would they scribble in their notebooks, what words could they find to tell what they were seeing here, on a world that was less than a name back home?

All the words had already been used so many times.

And he looked, too, at Derryoc, at the plump figure plodding through ruin. How could he see only problems here, in this city where even the dead had gone away? How could he see only house types and power sources, city plans and technological levels? What sort of eyes did it take so that you saw no ghosts? What kind of ears did a man need not to hear the whispers, the grief, the music lost and faraway?

Even as they were walking now, other men had walked, down this very street. No sand then, no jagged concrete ruptures, no decay and collapse and fire scar. Trees, perhaps. Green grass.

57

A buzz of commerce. A blur of faces: happy, sad, handsome, ugly. A news screen: words and pictures from around the world. What had been news to them, so near the end? What could they have been thinking about, talking about, joking about?

The weather tomorrow will be fair and cloudy, with light rain in the afternoon. . . . The Greens won the Silver Trophy today, on a sensational play by—— A man went berserk on his way home from the office; he knifed three dogs before he was apprehended, and explained to police that barking kept him awake at night. . . . The situation in Oceania appears to be more serious than at first supposed, but the Council says there is no cause for alarm. . . . We repeat that the weather tomorrow will be fair and cloudy, with light rain in the afternoon. . . .

Voices, faces, laughter.

Arvon stepped around a fallen wall and followed Derryoc toward the center of the ruin. Oh yes, he was imagining things, imagining the phantoms that walked by his side, imagining the shadows that passed behind gaping holes that once were windows. But the ghosts were real, ghosts were always real in these graveyards of civilizations, as real as the men and women he had known at home on Lortas, and as unseeing——

Cry for them, for they can sorrow no more. Cry for them, for they laughed and loved, and are gone.

"Here's the library," called Derryoc.

"What's left of it," said Nlesine.

"What a mess," said Tsriga.

Lajor snapped a picture. "Chapter Umpteen," he muttered. "For summary see Chapter One."

They climbed inside, their flashlight beams sending little tunnels of pale light into the gloom. Their footsteps echoed down silent corridors. Sand was everywhere, and dust rose before them in puffs and clouds.

"No sign of fire here," Derryoc said, pleased. "Look for

58

periodicals; they may have survived if it's been this dry for long. What do you think, Tsriga?"

Tsriga shrugged. "Not much sign of moisture. Probably dry since the blast."

"A good haul," Derryoc said. "Never mind the novels—see if you can find history books; check by the pictures. We'll just have to take tapes at random."

"Me, I'll take novels," Nlesine said. "Who knows, some poor guy probably thought his stuff would live forever."

For the first time Arvon felt some warmth for Nlesine.

What should you take from one library from one city from one more world of the dead? What words should you select for the linguists to analyze, for the computers to buzz over, for the newspapers to sensationalize? What lines could you find that would add up to one more footnote in one more history of man?

Arvon picked more or less as fancy dictated from the vacuum-sealed cases that preserved the old books. He had some knowledge of linguistics, enough to estimate what he looked at. Some of his guesses would be wrong, but anything he saved would be unique. Poetry, certainly. Novels, of course. And history, science, political tracts, and autobiographies, most definitely autobiographies. . . .

"Let's go," Derryoc said after what seemed only a few minutes but had actually been hours. "We've got time for some close-ups before we start back. Did you see that statue out in the square? Almost untouched, if we could just find the head."

"Probably buried in the sand," Nlesine said. "I don't blame him."

They went about their task while the warm sun blazed down the arc of afternoon. It was a good sun, and it did its job as it had always done it, unconcerned that its rays no longer lighted a living world.

They already had maps of the city, photographed from the ship, so they spent most of their remaining time inside the ruins of houses, preserving what little they could on film.

When they were through they returned as they had come, back through the littered streets, out again into the sand sculptures of the yellow desert. The wind moaned in their faces, blowing into the city, whining around jagged buildings and through black holes that had once been windows.

Into the airlock quickly, for night was falling.

The outside port hissed shut. The dry air of Centaurus Four was pumped out, given back to a world that no longer needed it. The clean, slightly damp air of the ship came in. The inner port opened, and they were back in the ship.

Shake the sand from your boots, wash the sand from your body.

Put on clean clothes, clothes that do not smell of the dust and the centuries.

"That does it," Derryoc said. "Another world in the can."

"Little men, what know?" asked Nlesine.

It was difficult to joke, hard not to remember. It was always hard after a field party came back. What were the odds now, the odds against their own survival?

A million to one?

A billion to one?

Try not to think about it. Do your job. Cry if you must. Laugh if you can.

"I don't wish to conceal anything from you," the Captain said. He looked at each of them in turn. "We had trouble coming out of the field for this landing. We may have trouble again."

No one said anything.

"We'll have to start home soon, regardless," the Captain said. "The only question is, do we quit now or do we try once more?"

Silence.

"You decide, Captain," Hafij said finally.

"Is that agreeable to all of you?"

Whether or not it was agreeable, no one spoke out against it.

"Very well," the Captain said. His short, taut body turned

60

back to the control panel. "We'll try again. Hafij, stand by to lift ship. Seyehi, compute our course for the nearest G sequence star. We blast in thirty minutes."

They were slow minutes.

The ship that had brought life briefly again to Centaurus Four stood poised in the desert sands, folded in a warm summer night. A city that had lost its dreams was only a deeper darkness beneath the stars.

The wind whined across the dunes, calling, calling.

A thrust of white flame, boiling.

A crash of thunder, shattering the silence, then hushed to a rumble that receded toward the stars.

The long silence came again.

The ship was gone.

chapter 7

FAR OUT IN SPACE THE STARS DISAPPEARED, AND THE NIGHT winked out as though it had never existed. The ship made the wrenching transition into the distortion field without apparent difficulty; the high hum again filled the ship, and the gray desolation of not-space surrounded it.

Even within the field, which had the effect of lessening the distance between two points in normal space by means of "folding" space around the ship, it took time to travel over four light-years.

Time enough to think.

The men in the ship—with the exception of the priest they always referred to it as simply the Bucket, never the *Good Hope*—went about the business of being themselves, presenting their social personalities to each other like so many suits of armor. But there was no man among them, no matter how flip his words, who did not carry a knot of ice deep within him, a chill that no thermostat could regulate, and no sun warm.

For the ship was searching, searching a galaxy as other ships had searched before her, and would search after her.

She was searching for hope, and there was no hope. Man had found many things in space: new worlds, new loneliness, new marvels.

But he had found no hope there, not on all the worlds of all the suns that sprinkled a summer night as stars.

It would not have been so bad, Arvon thought, if they had found no other men like themselves in the universe they knew. If they had sailed their ships out of Lortas and had encountered only rocks and empty seas and boiling lava—that would not have hurt them, that would only have meant that they were, after all, alone.

Or if they had but found the cardboard horrors pasted together by a generation and more of the innocents who happily constructed space thrillers for the young at heart—how wonderful that would have been, how gay, how exciting! Arvon would have welcomed that colorful fiction parade with open arms: reptilian monsters slathering after ripe young cuties, mutants who had no emotions coldly plotting the obliteration of the Good Guys with the Sense of Humor, hungry planets that were just overgrown digestive systems, waiting for spaceships as a starving man might await a tin can——

Better still, if only they had encountered the noble princes and beautiful princesses and nasty old prime ministers of Other Worlds, or even a galactic civilization of swell old geniuses, waiting to take the brash young people of Lortas by the hand, and eager to lead their immature steps into a Promised Land of togas and fountains and bubbles and Big Clean Thoughts . . .

But the ships had gone out, and space was no longer a dream.

Dreams could be fun, even nightmares.

Reality was different, and it hurt.

When the distortion field had been perfected, making possible interstellar flight in a matter of months instead of generations, the first exploring ships had gone out eagerly, confidently. Sure, they were armed to the teeth, ready for the monsters their myths had prepared them for, but they were ready, too, for men of their own kind. They were drilled, trained, disciplined. There would be no awkward incidents, no sophomoric misunderstandings that might lead to disaster. They were looking for friends, not enemies. Somewhere out there, they argued, somewhere in that vast starry universe that was their home, there would be other men, other intelligences, other civilizations.

The people of Lortas were not fools. They knew, even at the start, that one world alone was only a tiny fraction of the worlds that must exist. Just as an isolated island, completely cut off from contact with other islands and other continents, must develop a less complex culture than those areas situated at the crossroads of the world, so must a planet alone amount to far less than a planet that was a part of something bigger.

Cultures grow through contact with other cultures.

No great civilization ever grew in just one sealed area, with only its own ideas to keep it going.

Fresh viewpoints, new ideas, different historical traditions —these were the ingredients that made for greatness. Here a people learned to smelt metal, there a culture hit upon electricity, somewhere else a boy found a light wood and played with a glider, still elsewhere a tinkerer built an internal combustion engine. Separate, apart, they were gadgets. Together, combined, they were aircraft that freed man from the rocks and the land, gave him the sky for his own.

Alone, a planet could go so far, and no further. There is a point at which a culture exhausts itself, no matter how rich and varied it may be. There is a time when it—stops.

Not dies, perhaps.

But life is a process. It means change, development, challenge. When it merely repeats itself, when it only survives, it becomes at best insignificant, and sooner or later the effort is too much, and it is extinct.

There comes a time, too, in the history of civilizations when technology is not enough, when gadgets no longer satisfy. There comes a time when science itself can be seen in perspective, a method, a technique, that cannot supply *all* the answers.

And man is not only the animal with language.

He is the animal who asks questions—constantly, incessantly. He asks questions as soon as he can speak, he asks questions as long as he lives. When men no longer question, when they are complacent enough to believe that they *know,* they are through. They may eat, work, sleep, go through the routine. But they are through.

The people of Lortas were still asking questions, but they were tougher questions than they had asked when Lortas was a young world. They knew there were no ultimate, final answers, but they were alive enough to want to keep trying.

Questions sent the men of Lortas out to the stars.

Not rare metals, not national defense, not even science in the strict sense of the word.

Questions.

Old questions, in a way, though asked in a new form. Old longings, old hopes, old dreams. What lies over yonder, behind the mountains? What lands may be found on the other side of the sea, beyond the edge of the world? Does the sun shine there, and do warm breezes blow? Would we be happy there, see new things, dream new dreams?

So the men of Lortas locked their bodies in shining cylinders and flamed and thundered outward into the great night. Not all of them, of course. Most people anywhere are content with whatever they have; change is too much trouble. But many of them went, at first, with a calm efficiency that could not hide the hope in their eyes.

They went out, and they looked, and many of them came back.

That was the end of the dream.

That was the beginning of horror.

They found other men, men like themselves.

There must be some mistake, said the people back home when the reports began coming in. *They can't be men, not men like us!*

But the anatomists said: They are men.

The biologists said: They are men.

The psychologists said: They are men.

There were minor differences from world to world, but the differences were for the most part not important: a variation in blood type, in body temperature, in skin color, in the number of vertebrae.

Man was not a rare animal in the universe, and it was the height of egotism to imagine that he was. All isolated peoples believe that they are the only human beings in the world, and when a planet thinks itself alone, before the ships go out into space, it is difficult for the people on that planet to conceive of other human beings elsewhere among the stars.

Why, man evolved here! they told each other on a million worlds, nodding sagely at their own wisdom. *He is amazingly complex, the line that led to him was a long shot, an accident, he could never happen twice.* And they thought, if they did not say: *We are wonderful, we can be found only here on this wonderful world of ours. This planet we live on has been singled out by Creation as the one, the only, and the original home of Great Big Adorable Us.*

Some just knew this to be true; others fiddled with statistics. They all ignored the supreme fact: they were taking a sample of one, their own speck of dust, and generalizing from it to the entire universe. Moreover, they were generalizing in an asinine way, for the one planet they had in their sample *had* evolved human life, and that made it unanimous, as far as they actually knew.

It was not that man was foreordained, built in from the beginning. It was simply that the evolution of intelligence, of the ability to develop culturally, necessarily proceeded along the road of trial and error, change and modification. A culture-bearing animal had to be warm-blooded, for he needed the energy, he had to be big-brained, he had to have free hands and specialized feet. A manlike form was the mechanical answer to one trend of evolution, and if conditions permitted he came along sooner or later.

So there were men, men like the men of Lortas.

Yes, thought Arvon, *and what had happened to these men?*

The reports came in, brought home by ships across the light-years. For a short time, a very short time, there seemed to be little consistency to the reports. Then the pattern emerged, and was only repeated, as the number of reports grew to a hundred, to five hundred, to a thousand.

The pattern?

Well, stripped of its technical language, it boiled down to something elementary, something frightful in its very simplicity. The ships had discovered three kinds of planets that had developed men. On one type the men had not yet advanced to a state of technological development that gave them a chance to destroy themselves. On a second type, above the primitive level but not yet to the level of space flight, men were organized into groups, busily hacking away at each other with whatever weapons they could muster. On these worlds the visitors from Lortas were received with suspicion, with hostility, with fear. Their ships were impounded, their knowledge was used to fight in wars that were utterly meaningless to them. Crews that landed on these worlds seldom got home again.

And there was a third type, of which Centaurus Four was a good example. On these worlds man had evolved, he had developed weapons powerful enough to do the job, and he was extinct. The methods varied: germs, crop blights, cobalt bombs, gas. The result was the same: extinction.

In all the universe they could reach, this was what had become of man. As soon as he was able to do it he destroyed himself.

Ho, friend and neighbor!

Many thanks for the inspiring example you have set for us! *And us, what of us? Are we not men, the same as they were?*

That, indeed, was the catch. The civilization of Lortas was an old civilization, and thought of itself as sophisticated. It had weathered many a storm and it had survived. The people had always felt a certain pride in this, and suddenly they had evidence to show them how right—or how foolish—this pride was.

For Lortas, alone of all the worlds in the known universe, had spawned man, watched him develop a mighty technology, and lived to tell the tale.

At first, even for a sophisticated people, this was a boost for the ego. They, and they alone, had mastered the art of living with each other in peace, and even in friendship.

We're different!

We've succeeded!

We're better than they are, smarter, wiser!

There was a religious revival, a time of thanksgiving. The inevitable cults appeared, the inexorable political philosophies: Let's pull in our horns, stay at home, live our own lives. Let's rejoice in our own goodness, keep away from other men, cultivate our own garden. Why?

Because we're different, unique, better!

Aren't we?

Aren't we?

The initial unthinking smugness could not last. It was a frail balloon at best, easily punctured by factual needles. And the facts were not pleasant. When all due allowances were made, when logic had been twisted until it could bend no more, the truth was still there.

Out of a thousand and more worlds of men, *all* had perished as soon as they were capable of it. There were no exceptions.

And the men were the same everywhere, the same in the things that counted.

The men of Lortas were *not* different.

True, they had survived. They had survived for three hundred years after they had controlled their first atomic reactor. They had patched up their differences, there had been no wars. They *knew* that wars were obsolete when the first atomic bomb became possible, they *knew* that wars, ultimately, meant suicide.

But other peoples had known it too.

The books taken from shattered libraries on lifeless planets were full of it.

They had known, and they were gone.

Question: Is three hundred years long enough to let us relax?

Question: Is man of necessity self-destructive?

Question: If we go on living alone, never find another civilization to build with, what will become of us?

These questions were too tough for individual minds, but they were not too tough for computers. The data were fed in, the questions asked. The answers?

Other peoples had lasted three hundred years after harnessing the atom, but they had gone under eventually.

The odds were that man would always destroy himself. There was a chance that this was not true, but it was a slim one.

If Lortas built a figurative wall around itself, buried its head in the sand, its civilization would endure for a long time. It had gained that much by living past its first great crisis period. It might go on for thirty thousand years, but it would gradually slow, lose its vitality, stop.

One day it would be gone.

What can we do?

The analysis of the data showed one possibility. No human culture on record had ever succeeded in finding and establishing friendly relations with another human culture on a different planet. If a world could be found where men were sane, if contacts could be built up between them, if ideas and hopes and dreams could flow from one to the other—

Then perhaps man might someday be more than just another animal who lost his way. He might be more than just another extinct animal who couldn't change when the times changed. Then perhaps man could play a fuller role in the ebb and flow that was life in the universe.

If a world could be found——

The ships kept going out. But they had to go farther now, into parts of the galaxy so remote that the suns were no more than numbers in the great catalogues of the stars. They had to go farther, and they found nothing, and worse than nothing.

The world they needed was well hidden, if indeed it existed at all.

And it was all very well to speak of a *world* that was in trouble, a *world* that sent out ships, a *world* that was afraid. But most people are not afraid. More than that, they don't care.

Thirty thousand years? My God, don't we have enough on our minds without dragging that up? Let 'em worry about it when the time comes!

Of course, then it would be too late.

It wasn't going to fade away like a mirage.

So ships kept flaming outward, but their numbers dwindled. And their crews dwindled, too. A ship had to stay out five years in order to cover any area at all, and who wanted to go into space for five years?

Arvon thought of them.

Hafij, the navigator, was here because he belonged here. Seyehi would go anywhere he could be with his computers. And the Captain? The Captain was a driven man, Arvon was certain of that. But driven by what, and to what? Few men are motivated by vague principles and distant problems—it took something personal to get under your hide.

Derryoc? Well, this was his job; this was where his problems were. Tsriga? A boy, running away from an unhappy love affair, doing something romantic and exciting. Kolraq? His faith was tottering, he needed lumber to shore it up. Lajor? There must be more to the newsman than met the eye, and this was a long way to come for a travel book. And what made a man want to write a book, anyway? Nlesine? Who could understand Nlesine?

And himself, Arvon? Did he really know why he was here, why he had come?

No matter.

They were here.

And when the ship tried to come out of the distortion field, when it shivered and screamed and the lights went out, Arvon knew that they were in trouble.

chapter 8

THE DARKNESS WAS A TERRIBLE THING.

Arvon suddenly found himself without eyes, without a mind. He could hear a whine and screech of metal that ripped along his nerves. He could feel the sweat on his hands and forehead. He could sense his heart thudding against his chest.

But he could not think.

And he could not *see*.

In an instant he was a boy again, in a strange house. He was in bed, hidden beneath the covers. There is a wind, sighing through the trees outside the window. There is no light. There is silence, but a silence filled with sounds. There! What was that? A slither, a slide—a door opening? *His* door? Look out from under the covers, look toward the door! The noise again, but you can't see. There is blackness all around you. You hold your breath, close your eyes, and listen and wait——

And then he was back, no longer a boy. He felt the shrieking metal coffin of the ship around him, felt it jerking under his feet. He could see, but not with his eyes. He saw midnight around the ship, an ocean of midnight, an abyss of ice-flecked darkness, a black cavern with no beginning and no ending. He saw space lapping at the ship, trying to suck him out, set him adrift.

Space was very close.

A man forgot how close it was until his ship failed him. Then he remembered. He shuddered in the midnight of his mind, stripped of everything, even his personality. He was just a spark of life, flickering, trying not to go out forever——

The lights came on again, dimly at first, then with an unnatural white brilliance. The ship steadied. The chaos of screaming sound died away. The atomics settled down to an uneasy whine, far different from their usual comfortable throb in normal space.

If they had made it into normal space.

Arvon lay on the floor and felt life flow back into him again. He forced himself to lie quietly until he stopped trembling, and then he pulled himself to his feet. There was something the matter with the artificial gravity field; his feet felt as if they were encased in lead blocks.

Nlesine stumbled into the room, looking pale and wild-eyed in the naked light. "What happened?"

Arvon shrugged. "Don't know. We were coming out of the field——"

"The Captain said there might be trouble."

"I don't think he expected *that,* though."

"Come on," Nlesine said. "Let's see if there's anyone alive in the control room. Do you think we could run this buggy alone?"

Arvon laughed shortly.

Inside the control room the men were at their posts moving with a calmness that could not hide the tension in the air. Their faces were all curiously pale in the white light, and Wyik had a gash in his forehead that was leaving a thin trail of scarlet wherever the Captain moved.

Hafij was moving slowly from control panel to control panel, calling out a series of figures to Seyehi, who was punching them into his computer. The navigator's tall, thin body seemed crushed by the abnormal pull of the gravity field, and his black eyes were more concerned than Arvon had ever seen them.

Arvon checked the viewscreens with a quick glance and felt an unreasonable relief rush through him. The screens showed the black sea of normal space, which meant that they had gotten out of the distortion field, at least. He saw stars, friendly points of light despite their distance, and not far away a yellow sun burned in the screen.

The others filed into the control room and stood in a nervous huddle, trying to keep out of the way and yet needing, somehow, to be there, where they could see what was going on.

The strange hum of the atomics did nothing to ease their nervous systems.

The Captain hovered over Seyehi's shoulder watching the data come out of the computer. "Well?" he said. "How much time have we got?"

"Maybe twelve hours," Seyehi said carefully. "Maybe less."

Wyik turned to Hafij. "Set a course for the third planet, Hafij. We'll have to take it at full acceleration."

Hafij raised his eyebrows, but said nothing.

"Derryoc," the Captain said.

"I know," the anthropologist said. "Get set up for the standard approach."

"We *hope* it's a standard approach, friend. But there may only be time for a high-altitude circuit before we set her down."

Derryoc whistled. "That bad, is it?"

"Worse," the Captain said. He turned to the others. He stood there in his control room—short, powerful, unsmiling. His eyes were bright. Arvon would have almost argued that the man was enjoying himself.

74

"How much worse?" asked Tsriga nervously.

"Well, if you ever see home again it's going to be after a good long nap."

Tsriga paled, his young face suddenly very vulnerable. "You mean the field——"

The Captain nodded. "We got out of it by the skin of our teeth. We won't get back into it again."

"Are we okay otherwise?"

"You've got ears," the Captani said. "Listen."

The whine of the atomics shivered through the ship. It was a wierd sound, rising and falling, dying away almost to a mutter and then swelling to a scream that cut through you like a knife.

"Can we land if we make it to the third planet?" Arvon asked.

"We'll get down all right. The question is whether we'll still be in one piece or not."

The heavy gravity pulled at all of them, giving their faces a faintly grotesque appearance.

"It looks bad to Nlesine," Nlesine said. He said it without his usual glum enthusiasm, as though it were expected of him and he didn't want to disappoint anybody.

"I don't know much about that planet down there," the Captain said. "It looks like the best bet from here. I'm gambling on it because I have to gamble. If we get in close and find it won't do we'll try the fourth one instead. But it had *better* be a world we can live on, because it looks like it's going to be home for a spell. I think we can land. I'm not sure we can take off again unless we find a civilization down there that's able to help us out."

"You won't find it," Derryoc said.

"We don't need a technology that's actually managed space travel, remember. If it's just far enough along to manufacture some parts we may be able to sleep our way home."

Derryoc shook his head doubtfully.

Kolraq said quietly, "I'll pray for it."

For once no one laughed.

Derryoc went into a huddle with Seyehi as they got set up to scan for population concentrations and energy radiations. Hafij checked and rechecked his charts. The Captain stood still, arms folded, staring into the screen.

The bright, pale light cast a pallor on all their faces.

Like dead men, Arvon thought. *This ship is our coffin, and we're going to be buried in it.*

"Well, this is something," Lajor said, his voice a shade too high for comfort. "A shipwreck in space! Man, if they thought I was corny before, what'll they think now?"

"They'll think you were corny before," Nlesine told him.

"Okay, okay. Maybe we should have a drink on it."

"Just a little one," Nlesine agreed. "One for the road, you might say."

"That's not funny," Tsriga objected.

"It'll seem more amusing after six or eight quick ones," Nlesine assured him. "Let's go."

Arvon followed them out of the control room, more because he felt in the way there than from any desire for a drink. They sat in the comfortable green room, sinking farther into the seats than usual, and kept up a fog of conversation as though, somehow, it might serve them as a barrier against what waited for them Outside.

They had a few, but nobody got even faintly drunk.

The ship moved on, swimming through the star-flecked seas of space. A flaming yellow sun floated ahead of her, with scarlet gas prominences puffing out from its equator and then raining back into the photosphere.

The ship was a tiny thing, lost in the immensity of the universe. It was a speck of dust, and less than that. And yet it was not insignificant, even here. If the flare of the ship's atomics was only a dot of light against the furnace of the sun, she still carried life and hope and fear. The silent challenge she threw at the abyss of not-life around her was a comic thing, and yet in its way it outshone the splendor of the stars.

76

The hours passed.

The ship picked her way toward the third planet, intersecting its orbit as it swung about its sun. Outwardly the ship showed no sign that it was in trouble; it moved gracefully and serenely, a canoe in quiet waters.

Inside the ship it was different.

The third planet hung hugely in the viewscreens, a globe of blue and green that blotted out the stars. White clouds banded the world, looking astonishingly like breakers in a choppy sea. There was a glint at the poles that hinted of ice, and lots of it.

The ship screamed down into atmosphere, and the noise inside the control room turned it into a bedlam of sound. The atomics gave out their piercing whine, the computers chattered, the very metal of the ship itself groaned in protest.

"Four miles," called the Captain. "We'll cut across the equator, and then circle the poles."

Derryoc hung on to a chair that was bolted to the floor. His face was flushed, giving it an odd dark look under the white lights. "Get those maps. We'll need 'em."

Seyehi said nothing, hunched over his computers, his usually sure fingers clumsy in the unsteady ship.

The planet flashed by under them, a mosaic of continents and clouds and seas. The Captain stared at the control panels and found with something like scorn that he was holding his breath.

"Got it," said Seyehi after an interminable time.

The ship gave a perceptible buck, shuddered, and seemed to settle under them.

The lights dimmed, faltered, came up again brighter than before.

"No time to fool with it now," the Captain said, trying to speak calmly and at the same time having to yell to make himself heard.

"Can we go down and take a look from close up?" asked Derryoc.

"I don't know. Hafij?"

The navigator shrugged his thin shoulders. "We can try. It's taking an awful chance, Wyik."

Derryoc tried to examine the computer tapes, but it was impossible. "I say try it if there's any chance at all. It may be rough, but it won't be as rough as trying to walk around this damned planet to find out what's on it."

"If we can still walk after we get down," Hafij said.

"If we *get* down," Seyehi added.

The Captain made his decision. "We'll try. Hafij, I want to be able to count snow crystals on the mountain peaks and see the fish in those oceans. Skin her close."

Amazingly, Hafij grinned. "Hang on," he said.

The ship roared and slashed her way down, blasting through the high clouds with her hot metal sides hissing. She flattened out over the land, jetting like a river of flame through a cold blue sky.

She hurtled around the planet at a reckless speed, flashing over seas and islands and ice and vast green and brown plains. She roared from high noon into midnight and out once more into the golden sparkle of a morning sun.

Then she faltered and shook.

The drive broke off into a staccato series of blasts. The ship began to vibrate and swing sickeningly from side to side.

"No more time," yelled the Captain. "Strap in!"

With a thunder that made mountains tremble, the ship that had come so far stood on her tail and rushed down a geyser of flame toward her last landing.

Toward a green world, third from its sun.

Toward Earth.

chapter 9

THE SHIP CAME DOWN, SHATTERING THE SILENCE. BELOW HER a marshy rolling plain of tough grass and wiry shrubs and amazingly vivid wild flowers disappeared in a scorching cloud of smoke and steam.

The ship was coming fast, too fast. The braking jets were firing furiously but not accurately. The tongue of searing flame below the ship grew shorter and shorter, like a telescope slipping into itself. The noise was incredible, a blast of overpowering, crashing sound that rushed out and smacked into the plains like a granite fist.

For just a moment the ship stood poised, a scant few feet above the ground. Then she dropped with a sudden jerk, slammed tail first into the soft earth with a wet, shuddering concussion. She seemed to balance for just a second or two, and then she buckled and collapsed on her side. There was a muffled explosion, a flicker of intense white flame. Then sprays spurted out from the sides of the ship, sprays of liquid that threw puddles out in a circle a hundred yards around the ship.

The fires hissed out.

The ship settled, a broken, twisted thing dying far from the stars she had known.

Silence came back to the plain. Warm yellow sunlight flowed down from a blue morning sky, touching the reds and blues and golds of the flowers scattered through the clumps of grass. A shocked peace returned to the land, a hush unbroken by the song of a bird or the snort of an animal.

The ship was down, and inside it was very dark. After the whining roar of the atomics the quiet was a tangible thing, a hollow emptiness that was eerie and cold.

Inside the control room, sounds. A scratching, a cough of heavy breathing as someone pulled himself to his feet. A monotonous moaning, a continuous low cry of pain. A dripping of something liquid that patted on the twisted metal wall.

A light. A narrow white beam playing through the room, shaking a little in someone's unsteady hand.

A voice, low and choked.

"Where are you? Who's hurt?" The Captain's voice.

A shadowy figure struggled up, trembling. "Hafij here," the navigator said. "I think I'm all right."

The beam of light picked out a dark form slumped in a corner. The form did not move, and made no sound. The Captain made his way to the figure, shoving junk out of his way as he did so, and gently turned it over. He flashed the light into a man's face, then moved the light quickly.

"It's Seyehi," he said. "He didn't make it."

The moans could still be heard, helpless sounds made by an unconscious man. The light beam followed the sounds and spotted a body sprawled near the door that led from the control room. Hafij beat the Captain there.

"Lots of blood," he said.

80

The Captain studied Derryoc as best he could in the narrow circle of white light. The anthropologist's big frame looked somehow collapsed, and there was blood trickling from the corners of his open mouth. His weak cries were the sounds of an animal in unendurable pain.

"Derryoc. It's Wyik. Can you hear me?"

Derryoc did not move, and his eyes stayed closed.

"Hafij, take the light and see if you can get some painkiller from the dispensary. We don't want him hysterical when he wakes up."

"He's *got* to live," Hafij whispered. "Otherwise——"

"Here. Take the light. Get Kolraq up here, if anyone's still with us back there. Better keep the rest out until we figure out where we can put Derryoc."

"Should I tell them—how bad it is?"

Without thinking about it, Wyik and Hafij felt themselves as belonging together, with the others forming a separate group. Now that Seyehi was gone, they were the only ones left from the control room nucleus that really ran the ship. They regarded themselves as spacemen and tended to lump the others in the passenger category. In the old days the others would never have been aboard a ship at all.

"Better tell them," the Captain said. "They'll have to know sooner or later anyway. Tell Arvon to keep an eye on Lajor, in case he gets hysterical. I think the kid will be all right; this may be the making of him."

"If he's still alive."

"Of course."

"If only our two key men hadn't——"

"Derryoc's still alive, Hafij. Get the medicine. Can you tell from the controls whether or not the pile's dampened properly?"

"I threw the rods before we hit. I don't *think* we'll have a blowup."

"Tell the others you're *sure* we won't have one. The atomic jitters we can get along without just now."

"Right." Hafij took the light and fumbled his way out of the control room. It wasn't easy, since the ship was on her side and the door seemed to be jammed. He managed to kick it open and crawled through on his stomach. Wyik could hear him heaving something out of the way, and he thought he heard low voices.

Somebody was still alive back there, then.

He squatted in the darkness, his hand on Derryoc's wet shoulder, and sensed the hulk of the ruined ship around him. Somewhere out there past those twisted metal walls was a world, and they were stuck on it. He didn't even know whether or not the air was breathable, and he had no hope that the planet would be of any use to them now; the odds were overwhelmingly against it.

It had been his decision. He stared into the darkness around him and knew that he should never have tried for one more planet, one more sun. He had taken a calculated risk and he had lost. He had known the drive was risky but he had gone ahead regardless.

Why?

The Captain knew why he had done it. He knew that it had not been a rational decision. If only he could have forgotten what had driven him out in space in the beginning——

"Damn," he said.

It was too late now.

He heard sounds from beyond the door. Hafij was coming back, and he had someone with him.

"Well?"

"Good news," Hafij said. "We must have taken the toughest jolt up here—they're all alive back in the cabin. Just bruised up some, nothing serious at all. Nlesine hurt his left arm, but it isn't broken."

The Captain smiled.

"One more thing," Hafij went on. "The Bucket has sprung

82

a leak back there—fresh air is coming in and it seems to be breathable."

"It *has* to be breathable. We haven't got any power, and our air won't last long without purification. Hafij, it almost looks as if our luck is changing!"

Kolraq moved forward into the pale circle of light. "I have an injection ready," he said. "If you're through congratulating each other, maybe we can help Derryoc."

"Sorry," the Captain said, and moved out of the way. "Hold the light on him, Hafij—I'll try to rustle up another one in the supply room."

The priest examined Derryoc with his short, surprisingly sensitive fingers. He bared the anthropologist's arm, swabbed it, and injected a sedative from a hypodermic syringe. Derryoc still did not move. Kolraq wiped some blood away from his mouth and stood up.

Wyik maneuvered back into the control room with two more lights, one of which he gave to Kolraq. "What do you think?"

"We'd better not try to move him. He's hemorrhaging inside, and dragging him around won't help any. There's some stuff in the sedative that will keep down the infection, and that's about all we can do."

Derryoc continued to moan with grating regularity.

"Will he live?"

Kolraq shrugged. "That's out of our hands."

Wyik leaned forward intently. "Will he come to at all?"

"Perhaps. It's hard to say."

"He's tough," Hafij said. "He'll come out of it, Captain—I've seen them like this before."

Wyik nodded. "Come on. We'll have to get every scrap of data that came out of the computers before we hit. Didn't Derryoc take some notes?"

"I think so. He had a tablet——"

"Find it. Get everything set up. Kolraq, have we got something that will keep him free of pain if he comes to, but something that won't make him fuzzy?"

"We can try," the priest said. "But he should rest. You can't work him right away—that's inhuman."

"We need his brain," Wyik said simply. "He's the only one who can tell us what we've got to know about this planet. If we work blind we'll never get out of this—none of us, including Derryoc. That's all there is to it."

Kolraq hesitated, then wormed his way out through the control room door to see what he could find.

Wyik and Hafij settled down to watch and wait. Neither man spoke, but each was grateful for the other's company.

It was a strange scene, and Wyik knew it. The two lights threw silver rods across the jumbled control room, touching broken machines that loomed darkly around them. What had been the floor now formed one wall, giving the whole room a grotesque wrongness that no amount of logic could correct. Derryoc stopped moaning, but gave no sign of recovering consciousness.

This was my ship, Wyik thought. *We took many journeys together, and now the end of the line is a world without a name.*

Outside the darkness of the dead ship was a greater darkness, the darkness of ignorance. A land far from home, filled with the mystery and challenge of the unknown. Walk out of the ship, and you stood on alien land. Breathe the air if you could, and look about you. Blue skies, perhaps, and green fields. A river not far away, rolling cleanly down its gravel bed to the sea. And from that sea, if this world was similar to other worlds of its type, life had come. Tiny one-celled organisms and fish and amphibians and reptiles and mammals and, possibly, man.

What kind of man?

Wyik felt the darkness pressing him in. He had seen much of men, and it was not easy to find hope in the history he had found on many lonely worlds.

If men survived long enough, Wyik thought, they built ships

that lifted them toward the stars. That was a fact. But what led one individual man to ride one of those ships? What path did he walk that carried him out into the sea between the stars?

And how many men aboard this ship could guess at the secret that he, Wyik, carried within him?

The long hours passed, and still Derryoc did not move. He was breathing regularly, and there was no blood on his face. But—what if he didn't wake up, ever?

They had to take shifts, finally. Arvon and Tsriga threw together a cold and unappetizing meal from the synthetics, and Kolraq supervised a blood transfusion for Derryoc.

There was no panic. They moved through the dark cave of the ship with that heightened intensity of feeling that disaster brings in its wake. They talked quietly of Seyehi, and remembered that they had always called him Feedback. They found little to laugh at, but Nlesine kept up a constant stream of gloomy predictions that, surprisingly, made them feel a little better. Nothing could be as bad as Nlesine said it was, which was optimism of a sort.

No one left the ship. Without power the screens did not work, and they could not see the land around them. But presumably there was sunlight, warm sunlight, and then nightfall. They had seen a satellite coming in, so there would be a moon up there, floating against a backdrop of stars.

But inside the ship there were only shadows and pale light beams burning through the wreckage.

After many hours Derryoc stirred, whitened, and opened his eyes.

Arvon was at his side, waiting.

"Don't try to move, Derryoc," he said, touching his shoulder. "Just take it easy."

The anthropologist closed his eyes, then opened them again. His mouth was a thin, tight line. His breathing was shallow and choked, as though he had something in his throat.

85

"We're down," Arvon said. "It's all over. You got a sock on the head, but you'll be okay. Just don't move. Understand?"

Derryoc nodded weakly.

Wyik climbed into the control room, with Kolraq behind him.

Derryoc spotted the priest and managed a faint smile. "Am I ready for you?" he asked.

Kolraq hesitated. "I'm here as a doctor," he said finally.

Derryoc grimaced. "Don't feel so good, Doc," he said. "Stomach upset—like I was going to be sick or something——" He broke off, and his eyes clouded.

"Derryoc," the Captain said, "try to hold on a minute. We need you badly."

The anthropologist got his eyes back in focus. "Feel sick. Hard to think. Can it wait?"

"I don't know," Wyik said.

Derryoc looked at the priest. "How bad am I, Doc? Really?"

"You've got a chance," Kolraq said. "It depends."

Derryoc shut his eyes. "What do you need, Wyik?"

"The ship smacked down hard. It's not going anywhere again unless we can get help. We're down on a planet we don't know anything about. We don't know what we're up against, and we won't know if you can't tell us. Can you?"

"Big job," Derryoc whispered. "Sleepy."

Kolraq pulled the Captain back. "He can't do it, not now. What do you want to do—murder him?"

Wyik looked into Kolraq's eyes. His face turned very pale, and his breathing came fast. "Do you think that, Kolraq?"

"No. Of course not. I just meant——"

The Captain turned back to Derryoc. "Get some sleep, Derryoc," he said softly. "We'll try again when you feel a little better."

The anthropologist gave no sign that he had heard, but he seemed more comfortable.

"I'll stay with him," Kolraq volunteered. "I'll call you, Wyik."

"No. We'll stay together. All right?"

86

The priest nodded.

"The rest of you try to get some rest," Wyik said. "You'll be needing it."

The three of them were left alone in the wreck of the control room. They turned out the lights and sat in darkness.

Derryoc's labored breathing filled the silence.

"I hope he wakes up," Kolraq whispered finally. "I hope I did the right thing."

"You'd better pray harder," the Captain said.

chapter 10

THE ANTHROPOLOGIST SLEPT FOR EIGHT HOURS. IT WAS GROW-
ing cold in the ship, and Kolraq had arranged a blanket over
him, with a second blanket wadded up for a pillow. Derryoc
made no more sounds of pain. Indeed, save for the shallow,
rapid breathing that lifted and lowered his chest, he might have
passed for dead.

After the eighth hour they fed him intravenously. The sugar
solution dripped down the rubber tubing, and Derryoc seemed
to take it well enough. At any rate, his internal bleeding appeared to be checked.

But he did not wake up.

It became necessary to dispose of Seyehi's body, since they
had no way of refrigerating it. Arvon and Hafij put on face
masks, even though they were by now reasonably sure that the
air would not harm them, and went outside. There they dug a
shallow grave and lowered Seyehi's body into it.

Nlesine offered to stay with Derryoc. Kolraq and the Captain went out to say the words men say when death comes among them.

It was night, but after the gloom of the ship the vault of stars seemed brilliant and alive and compassionate. A silver half-moon swung over their heads and bathed the world around them in shadowed gray. They stood on level ground, as far as they could see, and the night wind was bitingly cold.

They saw nothing and heard nothing that lived.

Kolraq read the burial service in a steady voice, but his words were thin in the miles of moonlight. Wyik said what he could, and then the dirt covered Seyehi forever.

"He came a long way to die," Arvon said.

Now that he was gone, really gone, invisible under the earth, his loss struck home to them. The shock of the crash had worn off, and they were all suddenly aware that they stood very close to death and were far from the skies and the friends they had known.

It was strange to think that Seyehi would never again be a part of a control room scene, never again work with the computers he loved, never again smile gently when someone called him Feedback.

They went back into the ship and closed the lock as best they could against the cold.

"He's stirring a little," Nlesine called.

Wyik and Kolraq took their lights and hurried forward. Both of them tried not to think about the grave they had seen. But a second grave nudged icily against their minds. . . .

The anthropologist moved one leg suddenly. His eyes opened, and he strained as though he were trying to sit up.

Kolraq caught him, held him down. "Easy, old friend. Don't move if you can help it."

Derryoc was awake now, and awareness came back. "I must be half dead if I'm your old friend," he whispered. "You never called me that before."

"I——"

"Don't apologize. Thanks. I appreciated it. Could I have a drink?"

"Water?" suggested Wyik.

Derryoc frowned, a little color coming into his pale face. "I guess it'll have to be water. Never thought I'd come to it, though."

The Captain laughed. Maybe he was getting better, maybe he would even get well!

Nlesine brought some water, and Derryoc sipped it gratefully. But he stopped after perhaps two ounces. His face whitened again. He coughed convulsively, his body straining under the blanket. Flecks of red appeared at the corners of his mouth.

The spasm subsided, just as Kolraq was getting the needle ready.

"Better not try *that* again," Derryoc said, and smiled weakly.

No one spoke. Wyik was afraid to suggest anything, and Kolraq was desperately trying to think of something that would help Derryoc, even though it was becoming clear that the man was beyond his help.

Derryoc himself broke the silence. "If we're going to work, we'd better get to it."

"Do you feel well enough?" the Captain asked.

Derryoc looked at him steadily. "I won't ever feel any better, will I, Wyik?"

Wyik didn't answer. Instead, he carefully propped Derryoc up on the blanket so that his head was in a position where he could read without straining. Then he fixed three lights above and behind Derryoc, and slid a magnetized panel into place to hold the computer tapes and notes.

Hafij squirmed around until he was able to hold items up for inspection without cutting off the light.

"This is going to be very much of an impressionistic job," the anthropologist warned them. "Don't trust it too far."

"Your guess will be better than anything we could work out

on our own," Wyik said. "How long will you need before you can answer questions?"

"I *need* about a week to do the job right. I figure I've *got* maybe four hours before I conk out again. Do I have that long, Doc?"

"I think so," Kolraq said.

"Shoot some more stuff into me if you have to. All things considered, I think I'd better give you a preliminary reading before I go back to sleep—just in case. Let's say three hours on these tapes, and then I'll tell you what I can. Let's see that equatorial survey first, Hafij—it'll be coded A 14, I think. There, that's the one. . . ."

Derryoc's eyes were clear and bright, although his color was not good and his breathing was irregular. He showed no sign of pain, and seemed almost to be enjoying himself. He lost himself in his work. Evidently his powers of concentration were undimmed; it was quite obvious that the other people in the control room had ceased to exist as far as he was concerned.

The long minutes ticked by and became hours. Derryoc absorbed material rather than studied it; he could fix his eyes on a sheet for a few moments, then motion Hafij to replace it with a new one. He could not have explained the picture that was building up in his mind, a picture developed out of half hints and subtle clues that might have been meaningless to someone else. The configurations of continents and seas went into his calculations, as well as an occasional lucky bit of concrete information picked up by the camera scanners. Mostly he was guided by a lifetime of study about the processes of culture growth; he supplied data that were not actually before him on the basis of what *had* to be there.

After precisely three hours he nodded his head. "I'm ready. Can you cut those lights down?"

Wyik turned two of them around, producing a more indirect illumination, and turned the other up so that the beam passed over Derryoc's head.

"Do you feel strong enough to talk?"

"No. But let's not waste time being polite. You won't like what I've got to say, but you'd better hear it."

The others pressed closer, listening. This was no longer an abstract problem to them—it was a matter of life or death.

"First," said Wyik, forcing himself to ask the questions, "can we get help anywhere on this planet? Anyone we can go to and throw this ship together again?"

"No," said Derryoc. "There's no doubt on this point, Wyik. If you're looking for an advanced technology you've drawn a fat lemon."

"You mean there are no men? I thought——"

"Oh, men, sure. There are men here, although they're not very numerous yet. The trouble is that you're a bit too early. I may be a little off, but I'd say that there's not a single culture on this planet that's even developed agriculture yet. Helpful, eh?" Derryoc smiled a little.

"In other words——"

"In other words, you're in the middle of a Stone Age world. The men are mostly scattered in smallish groups, living by hunting wild animals and gathering wild plant foods—roots, berries, stuff like that. If you want to know how to fix a broken spear point you've come to the right place. If you want to know how to repair a spaceship you'll have to wait twenty thousand years or so and then ask somebody—except that somebody will have probably blown himself up by then."

There was a long silence.

"We're stuck, then," Wyik said finally. "We can't repair this ship, even for normal drive. As for a distortion field that might get us home again——"

"It's out of the question," Derryoc finished. "You haven't got the tools to make the machines to make the other machines that might fix your ship. You're not going to put this baby back together with a monkey wrench, you know."

92

"Looks like this is going to be home, whether we like it or not," Nlesine said. "There's nothing we can do."

"*Almost* nothing," the anthropologist corrected him.

"I don't follow you," Wyik said, frowning.

Derryoc paused, gathering his strength. Then his eyes became active and alert. He was clearly interested in the situation just as a problem, apart from any role he himself might play in it.

"What's the normal procedure for getting home if your distortion field breaks down and you can't repair it?" he asked.

Wyik watched him closely. "Compute the ship's course through normal space, set the controls on automatic, and sleep it out. But we happen not to have a ship, and no computers either."

"But you *have* got the sleeping equipment, right?"

There was a pause.

"We've got the stuff, yes," Wyik said. "It's nothing very complicated: an extract from the lymphoid tissue of hibernating mammals, coupled with an absorbent of vitamin D; a little insulin and some common drug derivatives that have been known for centuries."

The lights burned steadily in the ruined control room.

"It's powerful stuff, no matter how simple it is," Derryoc went on. "And why would you use it if you were suddenly deprived of your distortion field?"

"Simple enough," Wyik said, puzzled. "The ship can't exceed the speed of light in normal space—or in the distortion field either, for that matter. But the field has the effect of 'curving' space to bring two objects closer together; it's a kind of short cut, as you know."

"I didn't ask you for a lecture on elementary space navigation," Derryoc said testily. "I asked you why you would use the drug."

"It's an emergency device. It's the long way home if you can't get there any other way. Distances in normal space are enormously long, of course. You may be a hundred light-years or more from home when the distortion field conks out. At normal acceleration in normal space it may take you better than a hundred years to get home, and by that time you'll be dead. But the drug makes it possible for you to go into a sort of suspended animation; your bodily processes slow down until there is hardly a spark to keep you alive. When you get home you wake up—and even if hundreds of years have passed on the ship you're only a week or so older as far as wear and tear on your body is concerned. Of course, all your friends will be dead, you'll have to begin your life all over again——"

"But you'll be home," the anthropologist interrupted. "Don't be so long-winded, Wyik; there's no time for that."

"I still don't get it," Hafij said. "We haven't got any ship, and the people here are still in the Stone Age."

"Sure, sure," Derryoc said impatiently. "They're in the Stone Age *now* and so they can't help you. But suppose you had landed here fifteen or twenty thousand years *later*? What then?"

Wyik hesitated. "Probably this would have been a dead planet. As soon as they got atomic energy, they'd go the way the rest of them went."

"*We* didn't destroy ourselves," Kolraq put in, with more fire in his voice than had been heard in the control room for many days. "We set out on this voyage in the hope of finding someone else who might survive, someone we could talk to. How do we know—*maybe those savages out there will be the ones we were looking for.* It would be a lovely, terrible irony. . . ."

"The odds are against it," Wyik said flatly.

Derryoc coughed slightly, blinked his eyes, and went on. "For once, gentlemen, I'm with Kolraq. You speak of odds, Wyik, but you're not *thinking*. What chance do you have to get help from any other world but the one you're on?"

"No chance," Wyik admitted.

"Very well. Your *only* hope is with those people out there, those crude-seeming men hunting wild animals and starving half the time. Either they help you, or no one does. They can't help you now. Therefore you've got to wait until they *can* help you. Since you aren't likely to live fifteen thousand years or so you've got to use the drug—use most all of it—and sleep just as long as you possibly can. Then, maybe, you can go home in one of *their* ships."

"How do we know we'll even have a home to go to after all those years?"

"You don't. And you don't know, either, that these people will refrain from blowing themselves up until after they've developed space travel. But you're not going to throw a space-ship together out of mud and trees, I can promise you that. And you'll never have a chance to get home any other way. So there it is. Take it or leave it."

"Take it," Kolraq said instantly. "Take it!"

"I don't know," Wyik said. "It's a long, long chance——"

Derryoc coughed again, and this time there was blood on his lips. "Argue about it later. Hold up that map, Hafij—the big one."

Hafij held it up awkwardly where the light could fall on it.

"Listen closely," Derryoc said, speaking very fast. His voice was thin now, and hard to hear. "I may be wrong—I'm guessing from faulty data—but I've got some more advice."

"Yes?" Wyik moved still closer, looking worriedly at the anthropologist.

"The ship crashed *here*," Derryoc said, his finger reaching up to the map. He touched a spot high in what would one day be called Northeast Asia. "I don't think you should stay here if you can avoid it."

"Why not?"

"Too complicated to explain, Wyik. It's a peripheral area, for one thing—it's out on the fringes. That means the odds are against its developing as rapidly as some other places. There are parts of our own world where they've never seen a space-ship—you don't want to wake up in one of those."

"True enough. But——"

"Look at the map. Quickly, now."

"I'm looking."

"The most intensive development of culture on this planet seems to be *here,"* Derryoc said. His finger touched a part of what would in time be named France. "But there are people scattered all through this region, and down into this big continent here." He indicated Africa. "When agriculture develops, in my estimation, it should come first somewhere between these two major areas, at a sort of ideational crossroads. Perhaps along in here, near this body of water." He pointed to the Mediterranean.

"You think we should try to get to that sea?"

"No. That's where the population will be concentrated over a long span of time. Too great a risk of being found. What you need is an area that will be sparsely settled for many, many years—but an area that will blossom suddenly when new ideas hit it."

"I see that," Wyik said tensely. "But where *is* there such an area?"

"I can't be sure. I'm sorry, but I don't have all the facts I need. But this huge island *here* would not be a good bet—it seems to be mostly desert." His finger touched the island men would one day name Australia. His hand then swept over a number of Pacific islands. "These are too small, and impossible to get to unless you want to risk it in a boat you might make. But look at this."

Derryoc's finger traced the outline of the continental mass that would, thousands of years later, challenge the imagination of men as the New World.

"Is it inhabited?" asked Wyik.

"I don't know. It seems obvious that man did not evolve there on this planet, and there is certainly no great population there at present. I didn't *see* any men there on the tapes—but some few may have arrived. But look what's going to happen!"

The others looked, and saw nothing.

"Ah," said Derryoc in exasperation. "No time to explain. But some men are bound to get into that area—it's rich in land, well watered, enormous in extent. The men will come in from around where we are now—see, across here, down along here." His finger traced a path across the Bering Strait, down the corridor of Alaska. "In all probability, they are already filtering in now. They'll have a good part of this planet ahead of them—a paradise for hunters. But they'll be a long, long way from the cultural center of this world, which is away back here." He pointed again to Europe. "One day, when ships get good enough, men with a fairly complex culture will cross this ocean here, or possibly the other one; it doesn't matter. They'll find a virtually untouched land, and they'll take it from its original settlers. *Then* that area will boom, and that's where you'll want to be. You can stay hidden for thousands of years, and yet when you wake up you'll have what you need within easy reach."

The others stood silently in the gloom of the control room.

"Well, boys," Nlesine said after many minutes, "I guess we'd better slip into our old walking shoes."

chapter 11

THE EFFORT HAD BEEN TOO MUCH FOR DERRYOC; IT HAD EATEN up his last ounce of strength. While the other men still stood around him, trying to understand the words he had spoken, he drifted into an exhausted sleep.

Wrapped in soft darkness, Derryoc dreamed. Kolraq might have called them visions, but the tiny spark of awareness that continued to burn in the anthropologist rejected the idea firmly. He even smiled slightly in his sleep, so that those watching him wondered what he could possibly be dreaming that could seem funny at a time like this.

At first his dreams were touched with vanity, and he was annoyed with them. He saw himself through a child's eyes: badly hurt in a crash and yet saving his companions by the wisdom he had stored up through the years. In the fog of what was now a coma, the notion pleased Derryoc. He had never been a really big man in his profession, and he knew that the others thought him cold. It was good to be appreciated, to be liked. . . .

The picture faded. Equations danced through his mind, coupled with scenes from many lands and many worlds. He saw this curious animal called man as though in a many-sided mirror, everywhere a little different, everywhere the same. There was a flaw in the mirror, and he thought if he could only reach out, touch it, feel it . . .

Then he got better. The weariness evaporated, and strength flowed back into his veins. His mind cleared, and he saw everything around him with crystal sharpness. He was happy, very happy, for he had thought, he had been certain, that he was going to die. He was glad when they left the ship but he tried to show no emotion. What was he, a novelist or a priest, to rejoice in living winds and the smells of green grasses?

Still, it was good. The sun was a good sun, and warm, and it touched him with gold. It healed him as only the sun could heal. And then they saw smoke on the horizon, and the next day they heard sounds: cries, laughter, shouts. His pulse quickened. Men! He wanted to go to them, make friends with them, try to understand them. Oh, he would talk about data and statistics, but they came later, they were the rationale. For now there were only people, and fire shadows, and fresh meat and something to drink, something with a kick to it.

And perhaps here, too, he might find a man or a woman who would call him friend, who would make him feel just for a little while that he belonged. It had been so many years since she had died, the one who never should have died, the one who was going to live forever.

He was happy, as happy as he had ever been. The drink was good drink, it made his head spin, it was wet and warm and he could taste it in his mouth. . . .

Within two hours after he had slipped into an exhausted sleep Derryoc was having convulsions.

In three hours he was dead.

It was a dirty, messy death, with no touch of romance about it. There were no last-minute curtain speeches. There was not even dignity.

Arvon and Kolraq carried his body outside, and they buried him in a grave next to Seyehi. All of them felt somehow futile and lost when Derryoc was gone. There were words they might have said, little things they might have done for a living man.

For the dead there is only silence.

For Derryoc there was only the night wind under the stars, the night wind blowing always across a world he would never know.

The sun was high in the sky.

Arvon sat on a flat rock, his tall body comfortably slouched, his chin resting in his cupped hands. The slight breeze that rustled through the grasses had a keen edge to it, but the sunlight was warm on his back. There were patches of white cloud in the sky, and whenever one of them drifted across the face of the sun it grew decidedly chilly.

He looked around and discovered somewhat to his own amazement that he felt better than he had in years. The ship, a hundred yards away in the middle of a circle of scarred vegetation and scorched earth, was crumpled but harmless; in a few years, he supposed, it would be only a shell, and within a century it wouldn't exist. There would be only the plains, the gleaming-tipped mountains, the winds.

Maybe that would be a good thing.

He felt a curious joy just in being outside, where he could breathe clean air and hear the long, living silences that washed in from far away. He rejoiced even in the bugs that plodded dutifully through the grass, bound on pressing bug business. He was more than *ready* for whatever might come—he was actually *eager* for it, even impatient for it.

A man was not born to live in a tube of steel. A man was a

part of the land and the sky; his body knew that even when his mind reached out across the light-years, into star fields and challenge and desolation. . . .

He was lonely for his home world of Lortas, and the loneliness was accentuated by the fact that this planet was so much like it in many ways, even though separated from it by a gulf of years as well as miles. But he was not desperately lonely; Lortas could wait, would *have* to wait. He was not proud of the life he had left behind him there—it had been too easy for him, and it had come too fast. Too many pleasures, too many women, too many nights that were so similar he could never tell them apart. Even high living can get monotonous, he knew; the rut of the idle is a deep rut indeed. If his father had given him less, worked him more—but it was childish to blame it on *him*.

He thought, surprised: *There are places on Lortas very little different from this world I see around me. There are open fields under our sun, and clean winds, and patient stone. Does a man have to come so far just to find himself?*

"Fine thing," a voice said unexpectedly. "Here we are splattered on an alien planet, and you're asleep at the switch."

Arvon jerked back to the present and looked up to see Nlesine standing in front of him. The novelist's balding head was already pinkish from the sun, and his eyes had a sparkle in them.

Nlesine sat down on a handy rock, found it unsuitable, and settled on another. "Wyik wants to see us, whenever you're finished daydreaming. Big council of war or something. What're you brooding about?"

"Things. But I wasn't brooding."

"I know." Nlesine smiled—an odd smile, at once cynical and understanding. "You've been acting like we're better off now than before we crashed."

"Aren't we?"

"It'll pass," Nlesine assured him. "You're so glad to be alive you're suffering from euphoria. Very dangerous disease. Wait'll it freezes up around here—you'll stub one of your bare toes and it'll break off like a rotten twig." He snapped his fingers cheerfully.

Arvon nodded. "Funny, though—I'd never have thought I'd enjoy anything like this, even for a little while."

"Keep your eyes open, son. You can tell a lot about a man by the way he reacts to something like this. Take Lajor, now—he's the only one who's scared silly. He'll be trouble—you watch. Wyik is the same everywhere. Hafij is lost, I think. He was the only one of us who really belonged in space—Seyehi liked it wherever his computers were, but Hafij *likes* it out there. He'll get back, if anyone does."

"And the others? Tsriga? Kolraq?"

"I'm still working on them. You tell me."

Arvon shook his head. "Kolraq seems older than the rest of us, and Tsriga younger. I wouldn't push it further than that."

"It's the extremes that are sometimes the hardest to predict," Nlesine said half to himself. He stood up then, briskly, and dusted himself off. "Come on. It's time for Momentous Words from Our Noble Captain."

Side by side they walked back through the early afternoon sunlight toward the wreck of the ship.

They sat in a circle on the sunward side of the ship, out of the cold wind. They were very close to the two raw graves, and it took very little imagination to see Derryoc or Seyehi among them.

Even seated on the ground, Wyik dominated the group. He was by no means a big man, but he was the man you watched if only because of his tightly controlled energy; he was a coiled spring, ready to go at the slightest touch. He was their leader in fact as well as in theory, and he led because he was *hard*—not blind or stupid or in any way sadistic, but simply tough from the core out.

Wyik did the talking. "You all heard Derryoc, you know

102

what he said. He was the man best qualified to judge, and he advised us not to stay here. His reasons seemed to me to be good reasons at the time; they still do. But there are several questions that should be raised."

He paused, collected his thoughts.

"The first is this: Was Derryoc really in possession of all the facts he needed to arrive at a correct decision? It was a rush job, of necessity, and there were no computers to check him. He *may* have been wrong."

"His guess is still better than ours, Wyik," Nlesine said. "Mind you, a thousand-mile walk does not particularly strike my fancy."

Wyik smiled briefly. "I agree that his estimate of the situation is the best we have. If we ever want a chance to get home again, he's given us a blueprint that may work. There's really no other solution; there won't be another exploration ship out this way in a million years, and they'd never spot us if they came. Are we agreed on that?"

There were no objections.

"All right. Our problem is very simple, then. Do we stay where we are or do we set sail for that relatively uninhabited continent of Derryoc's? I'm sure that the point of this hasn't escaped you. We all know that the odds are overwhelmingly against this world ever attaining space travel, even in its most rudimentary form. The civilization here must be built by men, and we have seen, on world after world, that man characteristically destroys himself when he has the power. Those are the facts, and we can't ignore them. If we *do* make it to this other part of the world, and if we *do* survive a sleep of many thousands of years, there's a good chance we may wake up to a radioactive desert. If we do, that'll be that. There's a *chance* this may be the planet we've been looking for, the planet that will give us some company in this rather forbidding universe of ours. But it's an awfully slim chance. Is it worth taking?"

The youngster, Tsriga, spoke first. "You know, we wouldn't

have to sleep that long, would we? I mean, we could just go under for maybe five or ten thousand years—however long it would take—and then wake up in a civilization of sorts, but one still without atomic energy. We wouldn't get home, but we could *make* a home for ourselves." His eyes brightened with enthusiasm. "It would almost be like going back in time, on Lortas I mean, seeing all the things you only read about in history books——"

"I'll take the history books," Nlesine said.

"Your idea is worth considering, Tsriga," Wyik said, ignoring Nlesine. "And, of course, there's more to it than that——"

"Sure!" Lajor interrupted with sudden enthusiasm. "Why didn't I think of that? *We could just stay here.* We know what we've got now, don't we? It's not so bad, is it? I mean, it's nothing like some of the worlds we've seen *after* they began busting up the old atoms—it's green, you can drink the water, you can swallow air without searing your lungs out. We'll never get home anyway, so why try? We could build ourselves a little settlement, plant some crops, live out our lives. What's wrong with that?"

"No women," Nlesine said bluntly.

Lajor laughed. "There are natives, aren't there? What's wrong with them? We could go into the god business!"

"A god without guts wouldn't appeal to them," Nlesine said, smiling with one side of his mouth.

"What do you mean by that?" Lajor half rose to his feet. "Nlesine, I've had about all I'm going to take from you——"

Nlesine didn't even look at him. "Fearless Reporter Socks Effete Novelist," he murmured.

"That's enough of that," Wyik said. He did not raise his voice, but Lajor sat down again. "Let's not accuse one another; we've got enough problems without that. The fact is, Lajor put his finger on exactly what I was thinking. Mind you, that wouldn't be *my* choice, but let's be realistic. I'm not the Captain any more; I'm just Wyik. I can't order you around, and I would

104

be silly to try. The unhappy fact is that Lajor is right. If we just figure the odds, and if we believe that our only duty now is to ourselves, then we'd be better off staying right here. I think we'd survive. We might even have a good time."

"Vegetables don't have fun," Arvon said.

"How do you know?" asked Nlesine.

Arvon didn't answer him.

Kolraq, who had been silent throughout the discussion, got slowly to his feet and shielded his eyes with his hand. "Before we make too many plans about living with the natives," he said, "perhaps we'd better ask them what they think about the idea."

The others leaped up.

There, coming across the plains from the south, were dark figures. They were silent, but moving fast.

Men.

chapter 12

INSTINCTIVELY THEY MOVED TOWARD THE DARK PORT OF THE ship. Wherever he was found, whatever else could be said about him, man was dangerous. He was the supreme killer animal, and even his own kind faced him at their peril.

"Hold it," Wyik snapped. "There are only four of them. Nlesine, go inside and get some stun guns. The rest of you stay where you are."

Lajor moved a little closer to the port. He seemed about to challenge Wyik's authority, but he could sense that he would be a minority of one. "I think we should get inside the ship," he said. "We'd be safer there."

"But we couldn't *see*," Arvon pointed out. "What are we going to do—run and hide every time a hunting party comes our way?"

"Depends on what they're hunting," Tsriga said, smiling. "Stone Age men are often cannibals, aren't they?"

"The point is," Wyik said, "that we don't know anything about them. We've got to find out. I can't see any great danger —the range of our guns will be better than anything they've got."

"I hope you're not going to just open up on them," Kolraq said. "They may mean no harm."

"No one will fire unless we are attacked," Wyik stated evenly, looking at Lajor. "Ah—thanks, Nlesine."

Nlesine distributed the small hand guns.

They waited.

The four men who were walking across the plains were as silent as the wind. But they had a dog with them, and the dog barked a warning as he caught the alien scent.

Arvon watched the natives with a curious sense of awe. The figures moved closer, walking steadily and with no effort at concealment. He could almost make out details, but not quite. It was like looking into the past, staring into that vast and shadowed fog that was the cradle of man on many worlds. Here were men who had never known cities or agriculture or writing, men of the dawn, men only beginning the long climb that might one day lead to the stars—or to oblivion.

The contrast between their experience and his gave to the natives a kind of innocence. They would know fears and selfishness and perhaps horror, but they had yet to discover the evil that was within themselves.

They came on, walking out of youth, out of time. They stopped some thirty yards away, and Arvon could see them now.

They stood in a line, silent and unafraid. The dog that was half wolf put his belly in the grass and whined, his pink tongue dripping with saliva.

The reality, as usual, was something of an anticlimax when you saw it up close. And yet it had its own drama about it, the drama of sweat and hopes and smells.

The natives were not tall; there was not a man among them who approached six feet. Their hair was long, straight, and

107

black. Their eyes were narrow and dark. Their skin was a yellowish bronze in color, and they were dressed in crudely sewn hides.

The men were proud. They stood quite still and did not fidget. They eyed the strangers with a frank curiosity, but with an assumed superiority that waited for them to make the first move. They were armed—two of them carried stone-tipped spears, and two carried a kind of throwing stick armed with wicked-looking darts.

Arvon caught a whiff of them on the breeze, and had to smile. For phantoms these men had a certain solidity about them.

"Kolraq," Wyik whispered.

"Yes?"

"Go in the ship and get four sharp knives from the mess. Then we'll go out there and see if we can make some friends."

The priest ducked into the ship as the natives watched silently. What did they make of the ship, how could they explain it to each other? Arvon tried to see it through their eyes. They would know it was not a natural object, but would they connect it with the thunder that had shattered their world a few days ago?

Kolraq came back with the knives.

"Let's go," said Wyik.

The two men walked slowly toward the natives.

The dog leaped up, bristled.

The natives lifted their spears.

Wyik held a knife in each hand, gripping them by their points so that the handles were pointed toward the natives. Kolraq did the same. To the natives the intent must have been obvious, for the two strangers were helpless before their spears.

"Nanhaades!" one of the natives called, raising his spear to the throwing position. *"Nanhaades!"*

The dog growled deep in his throat.

"Put 'em on the grass," Wyik said. "Then back off."

They put the knives down, being careful to make no sudden movements. They essayed smiles that were perhaps not remarkably successful, which wasn't too surprising under the circumstances. Then they backed away from the knives, pointing first to the natives and then to the knives.

The dark-eyed men were not stupid. The one who had spoken stepped forward, scooped up the knives, and stared at them. He tested the edge of one against the skin of his arm, and seemed startled when it drew blood. He held the metal up to the sun, watching it gleam as it caught the light. He grinned delightedly.

The others moved up to him, looking and chattering as though gags had suddenly been yanked out of their mouths. The one with the knives backed away from them, trying to balance four knives and a spear in his hands. The three natives without knives followed him, talking rapidly. Obviously the leader was disposed to keep the knives for himself—and equally obviously the others weren't too keen on the idea.

A first-rate wrangle promptly developed, and stopped only when the man with the knives, after trying in vain to decide which one was the best, divided them up. Then they all got to laughing and reflecting sunlight into each other's eyes with the shining metal blades.

It was good fun, and Arvon found himself enjoying it hugely from a distance. He sneaked a look around him, and saw that even Wyik had a smile on his face.

Nlesine caught his eye and winked. "It looks good to Nlesine," he said.

And then, incredibly, the four natives simply turned their backs on the ship and walked away, with the dog bounding on ahead of them. They didn't look back at all, and appeared utterly unconcerned.

Soon they were only shadows again, and then they were lost from view.

"Well I'll be damned," Nlesine said, grinning wryly. "What do they think this is—a supply dump?"

"I guess we're not as important as we thought we were," Kolraq said. "We've just had a lesson in ego deflation."

Wyik shook his head. "They'll be back."

"How do you know?" asked Kolraq.

Wyik suddenly looked older, as though a fraction of his tremendous energy had momentarily deserted him. "They always come back," he said, "one way or another."

They slept inside the ship that night, and it was like sleeping in a tomb. The silence there was the silence that waits under the earth, and even the dreams were dark.

They posted no guard: once the air lock was shut nothing could get at them. But the ship had changed—in only a few days, it had grown old, it belonged to the past. There was not a man in it that night who did not think of that closed air lock with a feeling of unreasonable fear, as though he were sealed off forever from the sun.

Arvon and Nlesine had stretched out side by side, and they were both uncomfortable; the ship was pitched at an awkward angle. They stayed awake for hours, although they spoke only once.

"How about the scouting copter?" Arvon whispered. "Couldn't we take it instead of walking?"

"Maybe. I'm not sure just what the range of that thing is. It runs on power storage units, you know—too small for a bulky atomic engine."

"I don't understand why Wyik hasn't mentioned it. It's almost as though he's avoiding the subject, but we've all seen that copter."

Nlesine laughed shortly. "Mathematics," he said.

"Mathematics?"

"Well, call it arithmetic. How many men will that copter hold?"

Arvon considered. "Two, normally. But we could get more than that in if we had to."

110

"More, yes—but there's a limit. A quart bottle just holds a quart, no matter what. We might be able to cram four of us in that cabin—I think it would fly, but not well. Four isn't seven."

"I think it would carry five."

"Maybe—but what if it did? What about the other two?"

"Couldn't we make two trips?"

"Hardly. I know there's not that much stored energy in those units. It might be possible to just go halfway in the copter, but I have a feeling it wouldn't be too smart to split up at this stage. This isn't going to be any stroll through the park, remember."

Arvon yawned. "We'll work it out."

"Your optimism is a little sickening, my friend. I'll bet you actually believe we'll get home again someday. I'll bet you really think this is the world we've been looking for. It's too neat, Arvon. Life doesn't work that way."

"Sometimes it does," Arvon said stubbornly.

Nlesine chuckled. "Good night," he said.

"Good night."

The silence came again, a silence that blanketed the ship in cold breathlessness. As Arvon drifted into sleep, he thought: *It's quieter here than in the deeps of space.*

It was not a pleasant idea.

The natives came with the sun.

There was something almost supernatural about their appearance. One minute the plains were empty of human life, and the next minute men were there, as though they had simply materialized out of the grass and rocks and morning wetness. No, not supernatural, Arvon corrected himself—it was rather that they were *supremely* natural, a part of the land itself.

The natives brought meat with them, and there was nothing supernatural about that. They built a fire on the sheltered side of the ship, using what looked like dried dung chips for fuel, and roasted great chunks of red meat in the flames. The meat sizzled and dripped, and it was superb after too long a time on synthetics.

"A trifle raw," as Nlesine put it, "but what's a little blood between friends?"

They threw a piece to the dog, who wolfed it down gratefully, belched, and settled down to a sensible nap in the sunlight.

The natives did not seem concerned by the fact that they could not understand the language of the men who lived in the strange tower. Evidently they had come across groups of men before who spoke tongues different from their own, and it was surprising how well they could make themselves clear just by smiles and gestures. They certainly seemed friendly enough, although it was always possible that they were just impressed by the knives and wanted more of them.

Looking at the rippling muscles in their arms and legs, and the jagged points on their spears, Arvon preferred to hope they were merely congenial—and would stay that way.

When breakfast was over, the leader stood up, stretched, and pointed toward the south. There, across the plain, the land grew more rolling and a low chain of hills was visible, rising out of a purple haze. He pointed again to the hills, then to Arvon and the rest, and then back to the hills.

"He wants us to go with him," Wyik said.

"Probably got the old stewpot bubbling," Nlesine observed. "I vote we offer Lajor as a sacrifice."

"Cut it out," Lajor said nervously.

"Well, do we go?" Hafij asked. "Should we leave the ship?"

The four natives drew back slightly as they talked. They were not smiling now.

"I don't think it would be smart to refuse their hospitality," Korlaq said. "They mean no harm."

"How do *you* know?" asked Nlesine. "Have a vision?"

"I'm for going," Arvon said. "I agree with Korlaq—the more friends we have the better. We can close the port on the ship; no one could get in."

Wyik nodded. "We'll go. Take your guns, and let's gather up a supply of gifts—go easy on the knives, though. Maybe some clothes, a flashlight, things like that. All right?"

They got ready, clambering through the ship with an odd sense of sadness. Of course, they would be back, and the ship was a ruin. Still, it gave a man a funny feeling to leave his last tie with home.

The natives watched with expressionless dark eyes. They saw the men climb in and out of the black tunnel in the gleaming wall, but made no attempt to follow them inside.

When they had loaded themselves up and put on warm clothes against the chill in the air, Wyik nodded and pointed toward the hills.

The natives grinned, as though pleased, and set off across the plains. The dog was up in an instant and led the way. He didn't bark now, and kept his black muzzle to the ground.

The land was not as level as it looked, Arvon found. The grass seemed to cluster in clumps, and the black soil was rocky in between. There were hidden depressions that caught at your ankle and thorny bushes that scraped at your hands as you went by. Some of the bushes had brilliant red berries on them, and he wondered whether or not they were good eating. There were many flowers, poking delicate wet heads up out of the grasses. The air was crisp, clean, and cold.

The natives chattered among themselves and kept up a brisk pace. Nlesine was soon puffing visibly, and it was hard on all of them. The men from the ship were not used to walking, and Arvon found that he was developing a prize blister on his left heel.

"Trying to walk us to death," Nlesine panted.

"Don't look so weary," Wyik said. "We don't want them to think we're softies."

"We *are* softies," Nlesine objected.

Once they glimpsed a herd of animals ahead of them. They were beauties, large and delicately poised, with lovely brown

113

coloring and tossing antlers. But they were downwind from the men, and caught the scent long before they were in range of the dart throwers of the natives. They milled a bit, then a stag shook his antlers decisively, snorted, and set out at a trot toward the west. The herd followed him, not really running, but moving right along.

The leader of the natives pointed at them, said a word that Arvon didn't catch, and called back the dog that had started out in eager pursuit.

They walked for hours, and the men from the ship were playing out rapidly. Soon it would be no joke; they would *have* to stop. Arvon found that his mouth was so dry he could not swallow, and his chest was stabbing him when he breathed.

"Hail the conquering heroes from outer space," he muttered, and concentrated on putting one foot in front of the other.

The land began to rise, and they were suddenly on a definite path that wound into the hills. The hills, seen close up, were fairly formidable, and the rocks were worn and treacherously smooth, as though something heavy had ground them down.

They kept walking.

Behind them and to the west black clouds began to pile up in the sky and the wind moaned down across the plains. The grasses undulated in the wind like waves, and far off in the distance there was the rumble of thunder.

The natives kept chattering happily.

The men from space stuck their heads down and kept with it.

Even Nlesine, for once, had nothing to say.

Within an hour it was raining hard.

chapter 13

You don't notice scenery in the rain.

The water whirs and drums all around you, splashing on the rocks and digging tiny holes in the wet black earth. Your hair is plastered down on your forehead, and water drips from it and slides across your slick, shining face. Rain gets in your eyes, and you blink, and they get red and stingy.

Your clothes hang on your body like heavy felt sacks, and your own sweat makes you clammy and hot. There is water in your shoes, gallons of it, and every time you take a step you feel your toes squishing in your own private river.

The ground under you is slippery, and occasionally you fall down. You grab out for a tree or a limb to support yourself, but there are no trees. Soon your face is cut a little, and it stings where the rain hits against it.

No, you don't have much time for scenery.

Arvon didn't know where he was, and didn't care. He was wrapped in a tight cloak of misery, splashing along and half wishing he were dead. A good many of his romantic views on primitive life he left behind him in the mud.

Then, incredibly, it was over.

One of the natives ahead of him cried out, and a woman's voice hollered something in return. Arvon got his eyes to working again, and picked out a blur of warm yellow light in the gray haze. He squinted and saw some roundish humps rising up out of some sheltered high ground at the head of a small valley. They seemed too short to hold a man, but the party was making straight for them.

He stumbled on, and someone caught his arm and steered him toward a light. He was guided through an opening, and almost fell as his foot missed a short flight of steps inside. *Sunken living room,* he thought vaguely.

But it was light, and warm!

A fire. He clumped over to it, shook his hair out of his eyes, and held out his hands to the blaze. He was conscious of figures around him in the little pit house, and he heard some laughter. A small boy, he noticed, was staring at him with frank curiosity.

Arvon was quite close to collapse, and knew it. They must have walked a good twenty miles over a tough trail, and the plain fact was that none of them was used to that kind of work. Already, after only a moment or two by the fire, he could feel the tiny ache in his legs that meant stiffness within a few hours.

Still, a man had his self-respect.

Arvon dug around and found a smile somewhere. He used it on the dark-eyed, round-faced boy. The boy considered it dubiously, but finally gave him a broad grin in return.

"Ho for the outdoor life," a voice muttered brightly. "Hooray for open trails and the symphony of the rain."

"Hello, Nlesine. I see you survived."

"There are two schools of thought on that. Where's the hospital?"

116

Arvon shrugged.

The two of them stood side by side and dripped. The pit house wasn't big enough to hold the entire party; Arvon supposed that Wyik and the rest were grouped around other fires. It occurred to him that all of them would be duck soup for the natives if they proved hostile.

"I guess we're not as clever as we thought we were," Nlesine said, thinking along the same lines. "It's hard to remember, sometimes, that we're not on a spaceship any more and the rules have changed."

"Let 'em carve me up if they've a mind to," Arvon said. "All I want is a place to lie down."

At that moment the native who had led the party from the ship stepped into the room. He had on dry skins, though even these were spotted by rain, and he carried his new knife stuck in a kind of sash around his waist.

The native smiled and made chewing motions with his mouth. Then he pointed at Arvon and Nlesine.

"The import of your message is frantically plain," Nlesine announced as the native watched him blankly. "We are happy that you consider us edible, but must respectfully decline your recent invitation."

Arvon pulled out his gun. "Nobody's going to eat *me*," he said, forgetting his sentiments of a few moments before.

Then a decidedly haggard Wyik stuck his head in through the entrance flap. He saw the gun in Arvon's hand and his eyes widened in astonishment.

"What in the world are you doing?" he snapped. "Put that thing away—you want to get us all killed?"

"This joker wants to eat us," Nlesine said. Oddly, the words sounded a bit lame.

"*Eat* you?" Wyik stared and then doubled up with laughter. He clutched at his middle and got red in the face and short of breath. Tears ran down his wet face. Some of it was undoubtedly hysteria induced by weariness, but Arvon had never seen the Captain laugh like that before.

"I don't get it," Nlesine said, looking faintly hurt. "Arvon and I may not be the rarest of all delicacies, but I daresay any stewpot would be honored by our presence."

Wyik got himself under control. "Our friend here doesn't want to eat you," he explained. "He wants *you* to eat. In other words, he's inviting all of us to a feast."

Arvon put his gun away. He felt like an utter idiot, but he was too tired to care. "No," he said. "I'm out on my feet."

"No," Nlesine echoed. "Negative. Not going. Forget it."

The native grinned some more and chewed.

"We've *got* to go," Wyik said. He was weaving slightly as he talked. "This is no time to insult our hosts."

"A feast," Nlesine said with an absolute lack of enthusiasm. "Boy!"

"Maybe it'll last all night," Arvon offered grimly.

"Come on," said Wyik. "Time to kick up our heels and be gay."

One after the other, with the native leading the way, they went out of the pit house into the night and the rain. They sloshed along toward a larger structure, from which yellow light spilled out in long, warm splashes.

Someone was singing, and there was much laughter.

Arvon took a deep breath and determined to work on Having a Good Time.

Amazingly, it wasn't bad at all—at first.

As soon as he got inside the hot, steaming, hide-lined building, he saw a young girl who was sensibly dressed in virtually nothing at all. She came up to him, smiled, and handed him a somewhat squishy bucket-like affair that had liquid in it. Arvon, his mind reeling with exhaustion and the closeness of the air, felt that he had nothing to lose. He took a healthy swallow of the liquid. As he had expected, it wasn't water, and it burned.

Just the same, he felt better.

118

Even while a corner of his brain whispered that this whole thing was incredible and outrageous, he took another drink, and felt still better.

"Easy there, boy," Nlesine said. "It's going to be a long night."

Arvon nodded. He was sweating profusely in his wet clothes and wondering how many of them he might discard with propriety. Another drink, he felt sure, would settle the problem nicely.

With an astounding abruptness he saw things with that sudden tricky clarity that alcohol sometimes brings. They had all been cooped up too long in that ship, they had all been *serious* for too long. They needed a break, needed it desperately. They needed to forget, just for a little while. Yes, and they needed to *remember,* too—remember that being human wasn't all long thoughts and sad faces.

Arvon winked at the girl in what he hoped was a universal language, and it seemed to him that the years peeled away from him like leaves from an autumn tree. It was fun to be young, to forget. . . .

He knew that he was going to make a fool of himself, and he was glad of it.

The party was on!

Arvon went through the whole thing in something of a haze. It seemed to go on forever; event piled on event, and yet when he bothered to check he found that only minutes had gone by.

There was food, and plenty of it. Great slabs of dripping meat were roasted in the fire and served skewered with sticks. There was a kind of paste that was passed around in a wooden trough; Arvon wasn't sure, but it tasted as if it had a wild root of some sort as a base. There were berries mixed with animal fat and pounded into a tough, dry cake. It made you thirsty to chew on it, and that called for more of the warming home brew.

The fire threw great twisting shadows on the skin walls. Thin, tight things like tambourines with bone rattles were shaken and drummed on with fingers. Wild, joyous chants rocked the roof, and there was dancing that left you excited and exhausted.

Arvon was dizzy with drink and heat, and he was bone-tired. But he kept going on nervous energy alone, with that tense exhilaration that seems to carry you on forever. He felt a glow of good fellowship that made him everybody's friend and he was, in fact, having one hell of a good time.

Cannibals were very far away indeed.

He was aware of the others without actually watching them. Wyik was drinking politely, but his mind was clearly on sleep. He kept smiling, neither liking the party nor disliking it. He didn't seem in any way *superior* to it; it was just that it was nothing but an interlude for him, marking time.

Hafij had promptly taken on more than he could handle, had crawled outside to be sick in the mud, and was now comfortably oblivious by the fire.

Lajor wasn't having any, period. The newsman sat back in a corner, as far from the center of activity as he could get, and surveyed the scene with poorly disguised contempt. He drank as a man drinks to be sociable, which meant that he stuck out like a miserable sore thumb.

Tsriga was high and sailing with the wind. He was pouring out the story of his great shattered love to a middle-aged woman who couldn't understand a word he said, but who kept passing him the hide joy dispenser whenever he paused for breath.

Kolraq, oddly, seemed to be enjoying himself hugely in a quiet sort of way. He had cornered the local shaman and appeared to be trying to learn the native language. That was curious, Arvon thought vaguely—why bother with the language when tomorrow you'd be back at the ship?

Nlesine was in his element. Quite sober, despite the amount of lightly fermented juice he had swallowed, he was putting first things first. He had cornered a youngish, wide-eyed female,

120

and he was talking to her in an improvised sign language that was a model of simplicity and clarity.

All in all, it was a fine party. The tambourines rattled and the dancers danced. Gradually the fire died down, and Arvon thought he saw the gray light of early morning come filtering into the hide house. By then he was more than a little fuzzy, however, and it was hard to tell.

He didn't quite pass out. A girl helped him back to the pit house he shared with Nlesine, and it seemed to him that it had stopped raining. The earth was spinning under him then, and someone was tucking a fur blanket around him.

He did not sleep alone, but when he finally woke up the girl was gone, and he never did remember who she was or what had happened.

As a matter of fact, he remembered hardly anything when he came to and saw the sunlight streaming through the door flap. He had a thumping headache and he felt too weak to move.

He just agonized.

He heard Nlesine moaning something about a planet-sized hang-over, but it was too much effort to turn his head and look at him. He lay quite still and wondered if he was going to die. After a while he slept again, and when he woke up he was shaky but hungry.

He stood up, blinked his eyes, and decided he was alive. He was also alone, and he went outside to see where everybody was.

Judging by the position of the sun, it must have been late in the afternoon. Long shadows filled the valley, and he heard birds chirping. The village itself was soaking up the sun, and only a few puddles dotted the rocks to remind him of the rain. He took a deep breath of the cool, crisp air and headed for the biggest house in sight.

Inside it was dark; the fire had dwindled away to a heap of orange coals, and there were no windows. When his eyes adjusted to the gloom, he found Nlesine and Tsriga sprawled on the floor, awake but not eager for action. Two old native women were padding about, and one of them brought him a chunk of meat and a hide pouch full of clean, cold water.

"Wyik and Hafij are out hunting with the men," Tsriga said. "I guess we should have gone along, but I don't think I could even defend myself from the birds today, let alone wild animals."

"Kolraq's still talking to the witch doctor," Nlesine said. "He seems determined to learn the language; I can't figure out why."

"Maybe he likes it here," Arvon suggested, drinking the icy water gratefully.

"Maybe he's got a point," Nlesine conceded. "As a noble ancestor of mine once phrased it, this is no bad deal at all."

"It's worth thinking about," Tsriga said earnestly. "After all, we've got everything to lose and probably nothing to gain by following Derryoc's advice. This way we could at least live out our lives. If we take the long nap, chances are we'll wake up in one of those deserts where even the rats are poisoned."

"Better take a longer look around, pal," said Nlesine. "I'm sure it isn't *all* dancing and singing around here. Probably starve to death in the winter. Anyhow, Wyik won't stay—you know that. Duty calls, and all that."

"Well," Arvon observed, biting into a chunk of meat, "we won't go back to the ship today, anyhow—it's too late in the afternoon."

They didn't go back that day, and they didn't go back the next.

The natives were friendly, hospitable, and intelligent.

It began to look as though they would *never* go back.

Arvon felt the tension drain out of him, and the color came back to his skin. He was even getting a tan, despite the chill in the air. He was happy and relaxed and contented.

For the present he was more than willing to leave it at that.

chapter 14

When they had been there a week, Wyik called a meeting.

They all sat in a half circle on the rocks, facing him. They knew what he was going to say as well as he did, and yet the gathering was more than just a formality.

It was a turning point.

It seemed to be growing colder, and the men shivered in the thin sunlight. Below them, down in the valley, a small stream trickled along to nowhere, and it glinted like ice as it flowed. The few trees were evergreens, but they were dark now, almost black, and waiting for the winter's cold.

Wyik got down to business without any fussing around.

He stood up, composed but not calm. He could never be calm, not with his nervous system. He was always wound up, as though he might explode at a touch. He was not a tall man and yet, curiously, he seemed the biggest man there.

123

"Well, gentlemen," he said, "the holiday's over." His voice was not loud—you had to strain to hear it, but you listened. "I couldn't give you orders if I wanted to, and I don't want to. The fact remains that I didn't leave Lortas and spend years in space in order to go live with some tribe on a planet I never heard of before. I came here to find something, and I'm not quitting until I *do* find it—or until I'm dead. Our home is far away from us now, and maybe it's easy for you to believe it doesn't exist. It *does* exist. Some of us have children there, and there will be other children. I like these people here, don't you?"

The others murmured assent.

"Maybe—just maybe—*this* is the planet we have to find. Maybe this is the world that will make it, that will get into space without destroying itself first. If it does make it, thousands of years in the future, *Lortas must know*. A civilization cannot endure in isolation; we know that. If this world gets into space, and if we're not there to direct those ships to Lortas—the odds are that they will never find each other. You have all given up many things, and it is not for me to remind you of your duty. *I'm* going back to the ship, and I'm going to carry out Derryoc's plans even if I have to go alone. I hope you'll decide to come with me, but that's up to you."

He turned and walked away from them, alone. It seemed to Arvon that the Captain was always alone.

The others sat in the failing sunlight and talked. Some argued one way, some another. But they spoke without much conviction; they were going through the motions. Kolraq excused himself early and went off to find Wyik.

Arvon listened to the men around him and knew they would go with the Captain.

They went.

It was cold and overcast the day they left the native village. The wind whistled down through the hills, and the women and

124

children came out to smile and wave good-by, and then hustled back inside their warm houses.

Arvon felt that he could always come back to this small spot, lost in time, and be among friends. Sure, they had distributed a lot of presents, and they hadn't hurt anything. But you could not buy these people, and they apparently really liked most of the men from the ship. Perhaps that was a good sign, but he could just hear old Derryoc snorting at the sheer wishfulness of the notion.

The same four natives led the way.

It wasn't as bad a trip as it had been the first time. Once they got out of the valley they had a downgrade most of the way, and it wasn't raining. They weren't uncomfortably cold as long as they kept moving, and they never stopped for long.

From some of the high ground they could see far out over the plains, where the tall grasses and the flowers stretched out in cold green waves, like a vast inland sea. It looked cold and forbidding when the wind rippled it, and it wasn't hard to see it sheeted with drifting snow, with animals starving and the sun only a pale disc in a wintry sky. . . .

They could even see the ship, a shadow lying in a dark charred circle. It was miles away, but the clear air made distances deceptive. And, far to the north, they could see just a glint of ice clothing the mountains in chill white silk.

Glaciers, probably. A scant century ago might have seen them more widespread, although the sea of grass did not look as if it had ever been glaciated.

They kept a steady pace, and soon they were out of the hills, walking across the uneven land. Rocks bruised their feet and thorny bushes caught at their clothes. They could no longer see the ship, and there was no path.

Nevertheless, the natives never faltered, and the wolf dog padded through the grass with unerring instinct. It was very quiet, except for the rustle of the wind. It was warmer, though, once they left the hills.

They walked, and Arvon was pleased to find that he wasn't as tired as he had been the first time. It still wasn't easy, however, and he 'envied the natives their smooth strides and even, relaxed breathing.

He thought: *It's all very well to talk about walking halfway around the world, but we'd never make it. We aren't trained for it, we aren't tough enough for it. Not one of us would come through alive. It's got to be the copter, but the copter won't carry all of us. Wyik must know that.*

He watched the short, wiry figure of the Captain ahead of him and wondered. Did he know something that the rest of them didn't know?

The sun was sinking on the horizon before the ship finally loomed up ahead of them, and you could see faint stars in the sky. It was growing very cold. They would have to rip up some brush to build a fire; the wood was damp and probably wouldn't catch well. . . .

"Home again!" sang out Nlesine gloomily. The ship *did* look cold, like a tomb waiting for them.

It was at that precise instant, just as Wyik stepped forward to open the air lock, that a shriek split the air.

Suddenly the charred grass around them erupted dark figures.

Something burned at Arvon's shoulder. He looked back and was startled to see that there was an arrow stuck in his upper left arm. Warm, red fluid dripped down into his hand, and he recognized with a shock that it was his own blood.

One of the natives dropped, choking, with a shaft through his throat.

Wyik frantically manipulated the air lock open and fell inside. He twisted around, yanking out his gun, and yelled, "Get down! Hit the dirt! Damn it, Arvon, get *down,* man!"

Stupidly Arvon discovered that he was still standing bolt upright, as though paralyzed. He dived for the ground, wincing as the arrow shaft tore out of his shoulder. As though in a dream, he fumbled out his gun and looked for something to shoot at.

There wasn't anything. All he could see was grass. He shuddered. If someone knew where he was, there wasn't enough cover to protect a flea. He gripped the gun and tried to look in all directions at once.

He never heard a sound. But suddenly there was a figure over him, a stone knive plunging at his chest. He twisted out of the way and hit the firing stud on his gun. He heard the *choog* of the weapon, and then a body smashed against his face.

He struggled desperately, and then stopped quickly as he sensed that the body was a dead weight. He lay very still, hardly breathing, listening to the drip of his own blood. The body of his attacker was heavy, and it stank.

He heard cries and shouts, and once a scream of agony. *Can't lie here,* he thought. *They might need me. But if I stick my head up——*

Arvon squared his shoulders on the ground, ignoring the lance of pain from the arrow point still lodged in his shoulder. He got the body of the paralyzed man on top of him, and then carefully hoisted the head up until it cleared the grass.

Whack!

A spear cracked into it, and Arvon cried with horror as something wet splattered into his face. He dropped the body, slid out from under it.

Wait, one of their friends must have thrown that spear, and that meant——

"Hold it!" he yelled. Then he stopped. The native couldn't understand him! He shivered, then tried again, louder, "Nlesine!"

"Ho!" came Nlesine's voice. "Stay down—don't move!"

Arvon stayed down.

The harsh, convulsive sounds of combat faded. Voices filled the air again with friendly tones. Arvon got his head up, gave a quick look around, and then climbed to his feet. He felt pretty

127

good, considering. It had all happened so fast that he was more keyed up than afraid.

He *looked* terrible, though. His shoulder had bled a dark stream down his side, and he was smeared with the blood of the dead native next to him.

Kolraq ran up and threw an arm around him for support.

"I'm all right," Arvon said. "Better than I look, at least. Anybody hurt? What happened? Where'd they go?"

The priest smiled. "Nothing wrong with your curiosity, anyway. One of our natives—his name was Nanyavik—is dead. Wyik was hit in the leg, but not seriously. Two of *them* are dead."

"Who were they? What did they want?"

Kolraq shrugged. "I understand that there's much raiding between different groups in this area—it's the way a man gets prestige in his tribe. Our friends weren't the only ones who saw the ship come down, apparently."

Arvon could feel the stone point grating against the bone in his shoulder. "Just a little good, clean fun, is that it?"

Kolraq looked away, his eyes sad. "In their eyes, Arvon, it was something like that. They are men, after all. Our own ancestors on Lortas did much the same thing, and with as little reason, a few thousand years ago. The test is whether or not men know when to stop."

"Can you get this rock out of my shoulder?"

"Yes. No trouble there, I think. We can give you low-order paralysis, then dig the point out with a knife and sew you back up again. It'll be stiff for a while, but I don't think the arrow severed a muscle."

They started for the ship. It was dark now, but the natives were building a fire and there was already a pale glow of artificial light from a tube inside the ship.

It was cold, and Arvon shivered.

"I'm glad you'll be with us, Kolraq," Arvon said.

Kolraq smiled faintly. "I'm not going," he said.

Arvon looked sharply at him, but the priest said nothing more.

They patched up Arvon's shoulder and bandaged Wyik's leg. Then they buried their dead—three more bodies in graves by the silent, broken ship.

"This place is jinxed," Nlesine said. "At this rate none of us will live out the year."

The next day—cloudless but cold—Wyik told them what they had been waiting to hear.

"You men know that we cannot walk to that other continent that Derryoc showed us on his map. We're not strong enough. The natives say that other men have passed this way, heading north and east after the game animals, but never in winter. Isn't that right, Kolraq?"

The priest nodded.

"I think the longer we delay the less chance we have of making it," the Captain said. "I may be wrong, but that's my decision. So there's only one way to try it—in the copter. I'm not sure how far we'll get, or how well the copter will fly in a bad storm—it's only intended for short survey work, as you know. But I plan to go as far as I can in it, setting it down at night when we see a place to land. The copter won't carry all of us, and that's that. I think it will handle four of us safely, and five in a pinch. This is a pinch."

He paused, looking at them.

"Kolraq and Lajor are staying here," he said.

Nlesine frowned. "Hold on, Captain. You can't give an order like that." He moved forward, his face pale, breathing fast. "It's not for you to decide who's to go and who's to stay."

"I didn't decide," Wyik said slowly. "They did."

Kolraq nodded. "I saw this coming as soon as Derryoc spoke to us. When we got to the native village, I set about learning the language. It's no sacrifice for me, Nlesine. These people are close to the things I believe in—a unity of life, a oneness with nature. I sometimes think we have forgotten too many things, we civilized men. I want to stay and try to learn some of them back again."

There was silence.

"And Lajor?" Nlesine asked. "Don't tell me *he's* got religion."

Wyik looked at the newsman, who shook his head. "Lajor doesn't have to give his reasons," Wyik said. "It's his decision —and, frankly, Nlesine, it's none of your business."

Arvon looked at Lajor: sloppy, loudmouthed, friendless. *How little we can ever know a man,* he thought. *It's one thing to talk about staying here with all the others as a lark. It's something else again to do it for the rest of your life with only one other man of your own kind.*

"We're taking off tomorrow if we can get the copter assembled by then," Wyik said. "We need to pack the sleep drug *very* carefully, and some preservatives as well. Aside from that we'll need the maps and some food capsules. We'll take our guns. There won't be room for anything else—it's for Kolraq and Lajor, and the tribe." He paused. "Any questions?"

There were no questions.

They got to work.

It was a dark and dreary day, with shapeless gray clouds blotting out the sky from horizon to horizon. The wind was cold and even, but didn't pack much force behind it.

The little gleaming copter perched on the ground beside the wreck of the spaceship, looking very much like an odd minnow hatched from an egg carried by a giant defeated mother.

They shook hands all around, with Kolraq and Lajor and the natives who had befriended them. No one had much to say, and hopes were far from high. Somewhere above them Lortas waited, and a thousand other worlds, hidden beyond a blanket of gray. Somewhere ahead of them was—what?

They crowded into the copter and sealed the port. The thing

130

had a complicated lock on it, necessary in any craft that was used for exploration work. Hafij took the controls, and Wyik sat next to him. The others squeezed into the back.

"As long as nobody puts on weight, we'll do fine," Nlesine said.

The engine whined and kicked over as the natives outside watched in amazement. It roared, belched, growled. The copter blades sizzled over their heads, a circle of silver against the gray.

Hafij kicked in the boosters.

They were air-borne. The craft wobbled as a gust of wind hit it, but evened out and began to grab for altitude.

Arvon looked down. It was as though he stared into a well of time. There were the natives, skin-clad figures against the green of the grass. A dog, already ignoring them, nose to the ground. Kolraq and Lajor waving. Only shadows now, shadows on a rolling plain: brave and beyond time and forever lost.

Soon even the bulk of the wrecked ship was lost from view.

The copter climbed above the wind and came around toward the northeast. They saw a world below them, checkered green and brown and white.

Hafij set their course. The copter arrowed on, almost eagerly, toward a hope that was beyond hope, and toward an unknown land that men would one day name America.

chapter 15

THE COPTER WAS A FRAGILE INSECT, DRAWN TO THE SUN. IT hummed along a rugged coastline that bordered a cold blue sea. It was almost alone in the sky, but several times birds paced it for a few miles before falling behind.

The scene below them was one of wild desolation. Great mountains of ice floated in the sea, their peaks rearing up and glittering in the sun, their bases eerie dark shadows below the surface of the water. The coast was rocky and deserted except for nesting birds.

They saw no men, and there were no ships on the sea.

They flew for days and saw no animals.

It was a cold planet of the dead, and worse than that. Death implies life, and it was hard to imagine life in those rocks, or in the depths of that icy blue sea.

They spoke little. They just endured.

When evening shadows painted black fingers across the world, they set the copter down in sheltered coves and tried to sleep. But the driftwood made poor fires, and the frost bit at their hands and feet. Inside the copter it was too crowded to sleep.

They ate synthetics, when they ate.

The coast curved toward the east, a tongue of barren land licked at the choppy sea. . . .

There.

One great continent stopped, and another one began. Between them was a narrow band of shallow water—they could see the rocks on the ocean floor. It looked as though it were really one land mass and a playful giant had splashed a few buckets of water into a trough to cut them apart.

The water was perhaps sixty miles across, and was broken in the middle by some tiny forsaken islands. It was not a formidable barrier; there were undoubtedly times when a man could walk from one continent to the other on a bridge of ice.

The copter hummed over the water, and in doing so it moved from Siberia to Alaska over the Bering Strait, from the Old World into the New.

The copter turned and headed south.

There was plenty of snow, but most of the area was unglaciated. In fact, it looked very much like the country they had crashed in: essentially tundra, with great rolling belts of black earth, carpeted with grass and sturdy bushes.

They discovered something else. The mountain chains ran along a north-south axis, which meant that they did not constitute much of a barrier to land travel along their flanks.

"A funny feeling," Tsriga said, looking down over Arvon's shoulder.

"What?" asked Arvon, though he knew what the boy meant.

Tsriga gestured vaguely. "All that down there. If Derryoc was right, this part of the world is practically uninhabited by human beings. Just think: millions of square miles that have never seen a man."

"Yeah," said Nlesine. "We call them lucky miles."

Tsriga ignored him. "I mean, here we are, actually flying over the route that men will take someday—or are taking *right now*. I wonder who they are, what they're like? Arvon, do you think we'll *see* any of them?"

Arvon felt a thrill despite himself. The eyes of youth were better eyes than his, and they saw more deeply. "I don't know. Maybe. But I expect man is still a rare animal down there. We'd probably be lucky to see him."

"I hate to step out of character as a cynic," Nlesine said suddenly, "but what's that down by that lake? Over there, on your right?"

The copter buzzed toward a glassy lake. It was cloudy and hard to see, but there *were* dark figures in the grass, and they seemed to be in some sort of formation. They were drawn up in a circle, and several of them had formed a line as though to do battle.

"Wyik——"

"I see them. Hafij, can you drop her down a bit?"

The copter lost altitude, skimmed over the lake.

They saw the things more clearly now, and they were not men. They were shaggy four-footed beasts with horns. They stood in a circle, the calves out of danger, while the bulls tossed their heads and pawed at the wet ground.

A pack of smaller animals were howling away impotently, eying the calves. The smaller animals looked rather like the wolf dog they had seen before.

Very few of the animals took any notice of the strange silver insect buzzing over their heads. They were intent on their own business.

Tsriga took a picture, as he had been taking pictures ever since the ship crashed. It was developed right in the camera, and he grinned at the print, holding it up for the others to see.

134

The copter climbed back up the ladder of the sky. The little lake disappeared, along with the animals. They were soon replaced by other lakes and other animals.

It was a vast panorama below them, a world of water and earth and grass. The sky was a clean, cold blue, with a golden sun. The land was a patchwork of brown and black and green, ribboned with streams of glass and dotted with ponds that were blue mirrors reflecting the sky.

It was almost as if they were following a trail of grass into the south. What animals had followed that trail before them, and what animals would follow it in the centuries yet to come?

Darkness came early, and they had to land.

The copter touched the soft earth, the blades slowed and stopped.

They got out, listening.

At first, silence.

Sounds, then: the sounds of life in the wilderness, the sounds of a world men had not yet spoiled. Water chuckling over rocks, a snort from nostrils they could not see, a cold bracing wind that blew in from far, far away. . . .

Night was coming, but there was a moon.

Arvon stretched his cramped muscles and felt an unreasoning joy run through him.

"Damn it," he said. "I'm going fishing."

A pause. "I'll go with you," said Nlesine.

They rustled up some line, a cake of stuff to use for bait.

Then they set off, side by side, the copter forgotten, into the night, into the pale radiance of the moon, into the beginning and the ending of time.

Southward the copter flew, a dot in a lonely and cloud-streaked sky. And now the character of the land beneath the whirling blades began to change.

The barren lands of the tundra, broken only by lakes and stands of dark trees along the river valleys, gave way to a forest of stately conifers. The copter sailed over a sea of green, a cool forest that invited them with soft shade and damp mosses.

It was a hunter's paradise, teeming with game: caribou, deer, wild turkey. If you hovered in the blue sky over a forest pond you could hear the *slap* of a beaver's flat tail smacking the water.

And always the living silences of the big woods, a vibrant hush that was not emptiness but an amalgam of bird song and whispering pines and the pad, pad, pad of cunning feet. . . .

There was plenty to eat now. They simply spotted their prey from the air, shot it from the copter, and stopped for the night with their meat ready and waiting for them.

Once they thought they saw a man, dark eyes staring out of a green thicket. When they investigated, he was gone, and they found no tracks.

Once they spotted a curl of smoke from the air, but when they reached the fire only silence greeted them.

They flew on, into the south, and the country below them changed yet again. High plains rolled away from the mountain flanks, plains rich with grass and flowers, plains that undulated like the sea.

They saw animals in profusion now: lumbering elephants, a few wild horses, fantastic herds of big bison that blackened the plains for miles.

And they saw men, dark figures that hunted in packs like the wolves, stalking the herds with spears at the ready. Once they flew over a camp at evening, a rude skin shelter, a woman patiently scraping away at a hide with a stone tool, a child watching her solemnly.

Arvon stared at them, imprinting them forever on his mind. *You there!* he thought. *You, tired hunter, hungry child, working woman! Do you know you have conquered a world? Do you know that men like you will live and die for centuries, and then be replaced by men with guns from the other side of oceans you have yet to see? Do you know you have won a continent, and that one day it will be taken from you? Eat your meat, hunter,*

136

and laugh while you can! Tomorrow will be long, and a great night creeps from the depths of the sea. . . .

The copter hummed through the skies, over the sea of grass. The plains continued into what would eventually be the eastern part of the state of Colorado.

Then they headed westward, into the mountains. The copter slowed, an eagle searching for a nest.

Their power units were almost exhausted.

They landed high in the mountains by a tiny glacial lake.

One journey had ended.

The first night was cold, and the blanket of stars was remote and uncaring. They slept in the shelter of the copter since there were no trees.

Arvon lay on his back looking up at the stars. The air was crystal-clear, and he could see them plainly. There a blue one, there a red one, there one that seemed to pulsate as he watched.

He had gone through much of his life like other men, taking it for granted. Even the search through space had often not touched his soul with awe. And yet how strange life was, all of it! That sea of stars, those diamonds in chill black water. He had sailed that sea, and he knew that those stars were mighty suns, and around many of them drifted planets like his own, or like the world on which he found himself. Somewhere out there, in that infinite ocean, was there a man looking this way at a star in the night?

Hello, friend! Good luck to you!

He listened for a long time to the night sounds around him, the sounds of an alien planet far from home.

It was late when he slept.

In the morning, when the sun had climbed over the mountains, they fanned out over the area, looking for a suitably concealed spot for the long sleep that was coming. They worked down along the stream until they were well below timber line

137

in a stately forest of pines and aspens, but they did not find what they needed.

Well, there was no hurry. The fact was that they all subconsciously welcomed a chance to delay the injection of the drug. They fished and lazed around in the sun, breathing the fresh air, trying not to see the dead planet that all this might become. . . .

But they kept looking.

It was Arvon who first stumbled on the rock shelter. He had followed a little cut up from the mountain stream, and the dark shadowy slit of the scooped-out place in the rock wall stood out like black paint on white paper. He crawled inside and was delighted to find that there was a small opening in the back of the shelter.

He hurried down to the copter to get a tubelight, and he and Nlesine came back for a closer look.

The cave was nothing much—merely a hollow room in the rock of the mountain. There was a slow drip of water trickling down one side, and the place was damp and uninviting.

White bones gleamed on the floor; some animal had crawled in to die. Or had it been killed by something that lived in the cavern, something that would be back?

"I guess this is it," Arvon said. His voice seemed very loud in the silence.

"Swell," said Nlesine. "A granite bedchamber, complete with hot and cold running bones. Just what I always wanted. Know any good bedtime stories, Arvon?"

"A few, but they're not for children."

"Thanks very much."

They called the others, and after that it was simply a question of two weeks of hard work.

They stripped the vault of everything they could move to protect themselves against quakes. For the same reason they took tools out of the copter and carved themselves niches in the back wall of the rock chamber.

They arranged the tubelights, which would last virtually forever, around the room.

They took the preservative that all ships carried and applied it to everything they thought they would need: their clothes, their weapons, their notes.

They rigged a portal to seal the vault off from the rock chamber by using the gimmicked door of the copter.

They spent two days outside, doing things that were not strictly necessary. No man among them was anxious to crawl into one of those stone beds to sleep while the centuries whispered into dust. . . .

Finally, they could find no more excuses.

They went into the vault.

The last thing Arvon saw was the silver copter that had carried them so far. It stood outside the rock shelter now, its blades stilled, its cabin empty.

When next that portal opened, that copter would be dust.

The portal closed.

The men took their places for the long sleep.

Wyik sterilized the syringe. He opened the self-refrigerating duraglass container, which kept the drug sealed at a temperature close to absolute zero. When it was ready, he filled the syringe.

"I'll have to use it all," he said. "We'll go as far as we can."

"How far? How long?" The voice was Tsriga's.

"About fifteen thousand years." Wyik's tone was matter-of-fact.

Fifteen thousand years.

"Get on with it," Arvon said. "I don't want to think." *Don't want to think that no one has ever had to sleep so long to get home, think that this world may be radioactive dust when I wake up, think that I am afraid, afraid . . .*

The gleaming needle went to work.

Tsriga first, his lonely eyes frightened, then closing, closing
. . .

Hafij, his fingers crossed in the niche where he thought no one could see them.

Nlesine. He said it: "It looks bad to Nlesine."

Arvon. He was rigid. He fought it.

He saw Wyik inject himself. There was still a drop or two in the duraglass container—not enough to do them any good, not enough to put them to sleep for five years. He saw Wyik smile bitterly, reseal the useless thing, toss it on the floor, where it, too, grew colder and colder, refrigerating itself toward absolute zero. . . .

Arvon tried to scream, but it was too late now.

chapter 16

THE FIRE HAD BEEN REPLENISHED MANY TIMES, BUT NOW IT was only a heap of glowing coals. The rock walls of the vault pressed inward, muffling sounds, somehow creating an atmosphere of cozy comfort despite the barrenness of the cave.

They were all awake now, gathered about him, watching him.

The niches were empty in the walls.

Weston Chase shook his head, adjusted his glasses, and said, "My God, Arvon, I never heard of anything like it."

"It's true," Arvon said.

"Yes, I know it is. That's what makes it so hard."

Wes felt a sense of shock swelling within him; he couldn't shake it off. It wasn't easy to have your feelings, your beliefs, the very structure of your world, yanked out of their sockets, uprooted, twisted around so that nothing was what it had seemed.

There was no more horror left in Wes Chase.

Instead, he was close to tears.

"I think I understand," he said to Arvon—and to the others, although they could not speak his language. "It's—well, it's incredible."

Arvon frowned. "You don't believe me? You think——"

"No, no." Wes waved his hand helplessly. "It's just staggering, that's all. Not just the story, but *you*. You've changed, all of you."

How could he express it to them? How could he make them see, as he was seeing, with new eyes?

They were all so *different* from what they had seemed. He knew what it was like. That first year of medical school, at the University of Cincinnati. He had gone down from Ohio State, and he had hardly known a soul. He had looked around him in those first classes, and he had seen only strangers—cold, aloof, frightening. And then, years later when he left to serve his internship at Christ Hospital, he could barely remember how it had been, those first few days. Why, they were all his friends, or at least his acquaintances. He had studied with them, rigged skeletons with them, gotten drunk with them. They were no longer a sea of hostile faces—they were Bill and Sam and Mikowta and Holden. He knew them, he *belonged* with them.

And now, here in this strange vault in the Colorado mountains, it was the same.

The white-faced figure from hell that had chilled his blood that night so long ago was just Arvon—a man with a different background from his own, but a man he understood for all that. As far as that went, he knew Arvon better than he knew most of the people he saw every day in Los Angeles—and liked him better, too.

And the others, the ones who had awakened while Arvon talked, the ones who had wolfed down the food Arvon had gathered, the ones who stared at him curiously with those odd expressions of hope and fear and desperation?

142

He needed no introductions.

There, that man watching him with the deceptively sarcastic half-smile on his face. Nlesine, of course. He was balder than Wes had pictured him, and thinner. He must have lost some weight since the crash of the ship, Wes decided. Lord, had that been fifteen thousand years ago? He noticed Nlesine's eyes: shrewd and green, with just a hint of buried warmth in them.

And that tall, skinny fellow with the strange black eyes—that would be Hafij, the navigator of the Bucket. Yes, he saw what Arvon had been driving at about Hafij. The man had a caged look about him; he was not of the land or the sea or the friendly blue skies. His heart was out in the star-shredded deeps, his home was in steel and darkness. Wes disliked him at sight, but he admired him.

Tsriga. Wes almost smiled. He *was* young, hardly more than a boy. His clothes, subtly, were more garish than the ones the others wore. He was tall, gangling, knobby-boned. He was probably more nervous than Wes at this point. Wes felt a pang of regret—Tsriga was too close to the son he had wanted, but never had.

And the Captain. There was no ignoring *him*. Wyik dominated the vault without ever saying a word. He paced the floor with short, jerky steps. He reminded Wes of a boxer in the ring, waiting for his opponent to come out of his corner. He was taut, wound up, dangerous. He was more than just alive—the man blazed with energy. He didn't smile, not once. Short? Yes, but you didn't notice that. The overwhelming impression you got of Wyik was that he was *hard,* granite-hard, unyielding. There was a mystery about the man; he carried it with him like an aura. He was restless, driven, at war with himself. Wes watched him, and thought: *Watch your step, Wes. That man would destroy you in a second if he thought it necessary.*

Wes took out a cigarette and lit it. Ten eyes watched him do it. The smoke was stale in his mouth.

How could he tell them? He had journeyed with them between the stars, braced himself for the crash when the spaceship hit, laughed at the feast in the hide-covered pit house, stared down with them on a green and unknown land below the copter blades. . . .

It had been an odyssey that surpassed imagination, an odyssey that wound out of space and out of time, only to end here, in a rock cave in Colorado.

Only to end in failure.

He looked at them. Aliens? How stupid the word seemed now! A thing was not alien when you understood it. He almost wished that he had never gotten to know them, never shared their adventures.

Wes could not keep the sadness out of his eyes.

"Arvon," he said slowly, "there's something I must tell you, right now. It isn't easy for me to say, but you must believe that it's the truth. Arvon, *it was all for nothing.*"

Arvon stared at him, uncomprehending.

"We haven't got space travel yet," Wes said, hating the words. "I don't know whether we're going to blow ourselves up or not; I wouldn't take any bets on it either way. But we haven't got any spaceships, that's for sure. Arvon, you're stuck—all of you are stuck. It was a one-way trip."

Arvon stood up slowly. Stunned, he shook his head. He said something to the others in their own language.

There was a shocked silence.

"To come so far," Arvon whispered finally. "To take the chance, to wake up and find the world still alive, to hope, and then——"

He stopped.

Wes felt an icy shiver run through his body.

Wyik was walking toward him, and he had death in his eyes.

Wes backed away, his fists clenched. He knew desperation when he saw it, and he didn't propose to be murdered if he

144

could help himself. Something had snapped in Wyik; he would kill blindly if he got the chance——

Nlesine stepped out, caught the Captain's arm. Wyik shook him off, but by then Arvon blocked his way.

They talked rapidly, persuasively.

Wyik cooled off, his eyes cleared. He shook his head, disgusted with himself. He looked over at Wes and managed a smile of apology. Wes smiled back without notable enthusiasm.

"He's sorry," Arvon explained. "It is very hard for him—harder than for the rest of us, perhaps."

Wyik said something to Arvon earnestly.

"Are you sure of what you told me?" Arvon asked Wes. "I do not think you would lie to me—but are you *sure?*"

Wes tried to relax, but the strain of his imprisonment in the vault was beginning to tell on his nervous system. "You went to the town down there at the foot of the mountain, you looked around. Did Lake City look like a spaceport to you?"

"That means nothing. There are villages on Lortas that look the same way—sleepy, backward, forgotten. Surely, in your cities——"

Wes sat down, keeping an eye on Wyik, who was pacing up and down irritably. "We're close," he admitted, "but just not close enough. We used an atomic bomb in a war—oh, that was more than ten years ago now." He caught the look in Arvon's eyes and flushed. "We've done some work on rockets, I think —guided missiles and things like that." He flushed again, and then, annoyed at his own reaction, rushed on: "We *have* announced plans for an artificial moon of some sort, a little one they're going to shoot up into space. You could call it a spaceship if you wanted to, but I don't think you're going to ride home in it."

Arvon translated Wes's remarks to the others. There was a flurry of conversation. Wes noticed Nlesine's wry smile. If it had looked bad to Nlesine, his glum prediction had indeed been verified by time.

"These rockets," Arvon persisted. "You mean liquid-fuel arrangements? Powder? What?"

Wes shrugged. "I'm a doctor, not a space cadet." Arvon looked blank, so Wes amended his statement. "I don't know much about rockets. We have jet aircraft; I think they all use liquid fuels. No atomic jobs, as far as I know."

Arvon nodded dispiritedly.

"Wait a minute!" Wes snapped his fingers, and Wyik started like a cat. "We *do* have engineers, factories, designers. Why couldn't you tell them what you want—tell them how to do it—and have them build a ship for you? With your knowledge you ought to be able to cut centuries off the time it would take us to build a star ship under normal conditions!"

Arvon laughed. It was a short, staccato noise, utterly unlike him. He spread his hands helplessly. "You don't see the problem," he said. "It is difficult for me to make examples—no, that isn't the word I want." He paused, searching his memory. "It is hard for me to take *analogies* from your experience. But I can guess at some of the stages through which you must have passed. You have ships, large ships, for ocean travel?"

"Yes. We call them ocean liners."

"Well, then. Suppose you are the captain of an ocean liner and you suddenly find yourself on foot several centuries in the past. That date would be?"

"Around 1700, I suppose," Wes supplied.

"Yes, around 1700. As captain of a liner, you search out a shipbuilder and tell him what you want. Perhaps you even draw him a picture. Can he make an ocean liner for you?"

Wes shook his head, beginning to get a glimmer of the problem.

"Of course he can't. Now, with a spaceship equipped with an interstellar drive, the problem is magnified many times. Such a ship is built by specialists, with specialized knowledge. *We* did not build the ship any more than one of your jet pilots throws his plane together before he flies it. Wyik was our

146

Captain, but he couldn't design the atomic drive that powered the Bucket. Hafij was our navigator, but he couldn't give you more than a general description of how a distortion field works. If we had the ship now, we could take your engineers to it and *show* them some things; that would help. But our ship is dust now. The things we know might save a little time—cut out a few blind alleys—but that's all. If you have given us accurate information, your people are more than a century away from interstellar flight. The Moon will come sooner, of course, but it won't do us any good. We won't live a century more, Wes— particularly not after the effects of that sleep we had to take."

Wes waited, but Arvon seemed to have retired into thought.

"It doesn't look good," Wes said finally.

"You sound like Nlesine." Nlesine looked up at the sound of his name and bowed gravely. "But you're right. It doesn't look good for us—and it doesn't look good for you. This world you call Earth seems like a good bet to survive—it may even attain interstellar flight, as we have done. But then you can see what will happen."

"We'll go out into space," Wes said slowly, "and we'll find the same things you found. We'll feed the results to our computers—and then it will be *our* problem."

"Exactly. The odds against your ever finding Lortas are prodigious; it was only a lucky accident that *we* found *you*. Of course, I don't know that the Earth will survive; I don't know that much about it. What do you think, Wes?"

Wes remembered the paper he had read the night before he had gone fishing. He remembered the headlines, he remembered the talk he had heard at parties, in bars, in his office.

He remembered Hiroshima, and Nagasaki.

He remembered Hitler, and all the rest.

"I don't know, Arvon," he said. "I just don't know."

Arvon looked around him, at the bare walls, at the glow from the lights salvaged from the wreck of the ship. He was silent, and Wes knew he was seeing far beyond those rock walls, back into the gray mists of time. . . .

"A century!" Arvon exclaimed, overcome by the irony of it. "To sleep for fifteen thousand years—and to fail because of a hundred more!"

He turned, gestured toward the others. He spoke rapidly to them and showed them the notes he had made. He talked for a long time, and Wes caught some English words.

Arvon was teaching the others English.

Wes felt a hollow ache in the pit of his stomach. He was suddenly back in the present with a vengeance, and the effect of the story Arvon had told was wearing off.

Damn it, he was still a prisoner in this hole!

"Arvon."

The man looked up at him.

"You have no right to go on holding me here like this. My wife will be worried half to death."

Arvon hesitated. "We do what we must," he said reluctantly.

"You mean you still won't let me go?"

Arvon came over and stood before him. "I like you, Wes, believe that. But you are a man, after all. We know nothing about you except what you've told us. We've risked too much, come too far, to take chances now. You might lead an army to us, might drop atomic bombs on us, might capture us and pen us up like wild beasts. Such things have happened to men from Lortas on other worlds, with other men. We have not decided what to do with you yet. I promise you this: we will not kill you unless it becomes absolutely necessary."

He turned away and began explaining something to Wyik.

Wes tried to control a sudden fury. The arrogance of the man! Here he, Wes, had believed *his* story without question, fantastic as it had seemed. And now Arvon wasn't sure about Wes!

"Hell," he said quite distinctly.

And then he thought: *Suppose I were one of them, fighting*

148

*an impossible fight on an alien planet. Suppose I caught one of
the natives snooping around my hide-out. Would I let that
native get away, go back to his tribe, tell all the others?*

But reason could not help him now.

He was desperately homesick.

He thought of Jo, remembering her before she had been his
wife, and after. Her hair, like delicate silk when she pulled off
her bathing cap after a dip in the pool, her eyes that sparkled
when she'd had too much to drink, her laugh that he had not
heard in so long. He saw his house on Beverly Glen: rock and
redwood, and geraniums in the gardens. And green dichondra
glinting under the sprinkler spray. . . .

Jo. He couldn't keep his thoughts away from her, and not all
the thoughts were pleasant. God, how long had he been here?
What had she thought? What was she doing, now, this very
minute? Did she still love him, really? Had Norman——

No, don't think that. It isn't fair.

Is it?

He made no sound, but buried his head in his hands. He felt
the beard on his face with surprise. He closed his eyes, and he
was sick with loneliness.

His life was far away, and that life had not been all that
he had once dreamed it might be.

Somehow that hurt more than all the problems of all the
other men who had ever lived, or ever would live.

He slept, and dreamed, and cried out from the darkness
within him.

chapter 17

THE HOURS PASSED SLOWLY AND ROLLED UP INTO DAYS.

Arvon was working hard, teaching the others English. The atmosphere in the cave was one of utter gloom. Occasionally Arvon asked Wes for help with a word or phrase. Sometimes Wes co-operated, sometimes he sulked and refused to say anything.

Alternately Wes was fascinated by the situation in which he found himself and indignant at being held a captive. It must be at least October, he figured, and perhaps even later. When the vault door was opened, gusts of cold air blew into the chamber, and he caught the crisp, metallic smell of snow.

It was a long way down to timber line, and the tiny fire didn't really keep them warm.

They were, in fact, miserable—all of them.

Twice they felt the ripping vibrations of jets in the air over

150

the mountains. Each time the men from Lortas ran out of the cave and stared into the sky. They could tell that the jets were outdistancing their sound trails. But they could also see the stubbed wings.

For his part, Wes felt oddly displaced, as though he had been changed in some subtle fashion. He looked down at himself, at the old tennis shoes, the torn pants, the supposedly waterproof jacket with the rust stains on it. He felt the mouse-colored hat, which he had recovered, somewhat the worse for wear. He listened to the ticking of his watch, fingered the three keys on his key ring, felt the lump of his billfold in his pocket.

Many times he slipped the photograph out of its plastic holder and looked at it: at Jo.

She stood there, in her tweed skirt and brown cashmere sweater, looking at him, smiling a little.

Jo.

It hurt to think about her.

He came back to himself, wondering. Could this really be Wes Chase—a moderately successful eye, ear, nose, and throat man? A guy who liked to go fishing in old tennis shoes and a battered felt hat? A guy who liked to get tight once in a while? Could this be the Wes he had always known listening to talk about interstellar ships and sleeps that lasted fifteen thousand years?

The isolation of cultures, the destiny of man——

Surely, these things weren't part of *his* life?

Surely, spaceships and all that were things that intelligent people laughed at, like flying saucers. Fun to give you the creeps at a movie, maybe, but not part of the *real* world.

He shivered suddenly, almost seeing life as these other men in the cave saw it. Why, up there, beyond the rock, beyond the blue of the sky, there were other worlds, other men, other fears and laughter—and yet they were all the same, everywhere.

God, how ignorant he was! How ignorant they all were, here on Earth. How—what was the word?

151

Provincial.

They were hicks, country boys who thought the city was a myth, the world was flat, evil was a dream.

He shook himself, literally. It was hard to grow up. . . .

The really surprising thing about Arvon and Nlesine and Wyik and Hafij and Tsriga—yes, and about Kolraq and Seyehi and Lajor and Derryoc—was how familiar they seemed. Aliens? He knew men like them, like every one of them, in Ohio or Colorado or California. Supermen? Nonsense. They were just men, and he could understand them.

Understanding, he put himself in their shoes. Here they were, stuck on Earth. Here they were, and after years of searching they had perhaps found the one world in all the universe that could help them—but they had come too early. The ship had yet to be built that could carry them home again, and could do more than that.

A ship that could fuse the two great civilizations—a ship that could fertilize two great cultures, keep them going, give birth to a new, varied way of life that might carry man—how far?

But a ship that did not exist.

He knew what they were thinking; the same thing he would be thinking if their positions had been reversed.

Suppose he's lying? Suppose he's like too many other men we've known? Suppose he's tricking us, trying to catch us off guard? Suppose his people really have conquered space and he doesn't want us to know?

Or, more kindly: *Perhaps he means well but doesn't have the facts. He's just a doctor, they wouldn't tell him everything. Maybe there's some political reason why they don't tell their citizens what goes on. Maybe there's a war brewing. . . .*

Castles in the air, of course. But what else could they build?

Sure enough, in time, Wyik went to work on him.

"Your home, Wes. Where is it?" His voice was smooth, controlled, but there was a harsh undertone to it he could not quite conceal.

152

"They call it Los Angeles—that's Spanish, really, not English. It's a city in a place called California."

"How far from here?"

"Hundreds of miles. Too far to walk."

"It's a big city?"

"One of the biggest."

"They have many things there, Wes? Factories, technicians, scientists?"

"Sure. All that and Marilyn Monroe, too."

"Marilyn Monroe?"

"She's a kind of goddess who lives in Hollywood—that's a part of Los Angeles where they make dreams out of celluloid."

"She would be important to see?"

"She'd be worth a look, yes. Take your mind off your troubles."

Wyik frowned uncertainly. "Wes, we need your help. I know we have no right to ask it after keeping you here so long. But we—some of us—must go to this city of yours. Can you get us there without calling any attention to yourself? We want to trust you." He smiled. "But we can't, of course."

Wes thrilled, and color came into his face.

Here's your chance. You can get out! You can go home!

"It won't be easy," he said.

"I know that. We have discussed it thoroughly. It seems to us that the basic requirement is money. Can you get some?"

Wes nodded.

"Without communicating with anyone unless one of us is present?"

Wes hesitated. That *did* raise some problems.

"Think it over," Wyik said. "We'll give you until tomorrow. And think carefully, Wes. Don't make any foolish mistakes."

Wes looked into the Captain's cold, hard eyes.

"I won't make any mistakes," he said evenly.

The next day he went through the circular port, out into the

153

rock shelter. Behind him was the bare vault with the five niches cut into the wall, five rock beds where five men had slept for fifteen thousand years. . . .

Ahead of him—

Light.

White, blazing, blinding light.

Sun and snow, and the outward thrill of immensity.

He was free. True, Arvon and Nlesine were with him, and both were armed. But this was his world, and he knew it better than they could ever hope to know it. His freedom was his to take, when and if he wanted it.

If he wanted it?

Damn fool! Of course you want it!

Nevertheless, he turned and waved at the rock shelter: waved at Tsriga, trying to be brave; and at Hafij and Wyik, withdrawn and silent.

They all waved back.

"I know the way," Arvon said. "I'll go first, then you, Wes, and then Nlesine. Be careful—the trail is slippery in spots."

"So this is civilization," Nlesine muttered, his balding head pink in the bright, reflected sunlight. He picked his way over some rocks. "Kolraq had the right idea after all."

The stream was still running, chuckling blackly between banks of snow. Above them was the glacial lake, probably iced over in part, and below them, at the foot of an invisible trail, was Lake City, Colorado.

They set off at a good clip. For the most part the snow was thin and dry. They had to wade the stream several times, and their feet grew numb with cold. Wes was not in very good shape, and he puffed quickly in the thin air, but his excitement kept him going without tiring him too much.

Timber line, and black trees like burned stumps resting in the snow. Spruce and pine and aspen, patient trees, waiting out the winter. The air was cold, but it smelled wonderful, and as long as they kept moving they were warm.

154

It was late afternoon when they passed through the valley in the mountain foothills—the valley that had been choked with green and gold the last time Wes had seen it. Now it was barren and empty, with black rocks and clumps of brush like ink splotches in the snow. The stream deepened and slowed after its tumble from the heights, and it glided like oil over the comparatively level land.

There—that was where he had left his car. There was no sign of it now. It had undoubtedly been found within a day or two. He supposed that Jo had it—she had a key in her purse, he remembered. How many times had he locked his own key in the car and phoned Jo to come open the door for him?

Phone Jo. If only——

Well, they were still roughly two miles from Lake City. It was unlikely that they would see anyone, but there was a chance. A few hundred people lived there all year round, and there would be hunting parties as well.

"Better wait until after dark," Arvon said. He searched out a rock and sat down behind it, out of the wind. Wes and Nlesine joined him.

"I expect to freeze to death," Nlesine said. He sighed. "It would all make a dandy novel, but who would ever believe it? And old Wes here is too middle class for a good villain."

Wes shivered, and flexed his numb toes in his tennis shoes. It wouldn't be any fun to get frostbitten. He wasn't certain he cared for Nlesine's remark. "You've got things turned around, friend," he said. "If nothing else, you're guilty of kidnaping— and that carries the death penalty."

Nlesine raised his eyebrows, interested and not in the least alarmed. "You still have the death penalty? I wouldn't have expected it at this level."

"We've got it," Wes assured him.

Arvon shrugged. "We've nothing to lose. You're a funny guy, Wes—bringing that up at a time like this. Maybe we have a crazy man for an informant."

155

His smile took the sting out of his words.

Wes tried not to think; it was easier that way. The big problem, of course, was clothes. The odd dress of Nlesine and Arvon could hardly go unremarked, especially in Lake City. If they were seen, there would be talk. And then, regardless of their intentions, the men from Lortas might be crowded into a corner where they would have to fight.

In which case the outlook for Wes would not be bright.

No, he wanted no trouble while he was still in their hands.

But to get clothes he had to have money. Sure, they could steal some, probably successfully, but then what? Everyone would be looking for them, and there would be no chance at all of keeping things quiet.

"It's an odd situation," Nlesine said, idly packing a snowball. "Here we are, and we mean no harm to anyone. And yet there's no one we can go to for help. This culture simply isn't ready for our story. There *aren't* any men from space, as far as they're concerned. And even if someone believed us, what could he do? We'd get all balled up in local politics and spend the rest of our lives trying to convince the experts that we don't know how to make a death ray or a fleet of spaceships. These things have happened before, Wes."

"You *could* tell your story and show them where Lortas is on a star map," Wes said. "Then, someday, maybe they'd get there."

Arvon laughed. "You're suggesting we're not quite the disinterested altruists we claim to be? You mean we're worried about Arvon and Nlesine as well as mankind?"

"Damn right we are," Nlesine said. "I want to get home myself. I have no desire to be a statue—I've carted too many of 'em off too many dead worlds."

"Still, if you can't get back——"

"We'll do what we can," Arvon said. "But we haven't given up yet."

The sun drifted down the sky, and shadows lengthened over

156

the snow. The breeze died away, fortunately, but it was cold—
well below freezing.

When they could see the first cold stars they got to their feet.
They were stiff and sore, and they stamped around to get their
blood circulating again.

Then they hoofed it toward Lake City.

They kept off the road when they reached the highway and
ducked behind rocks when they saw headlights coming. They
could see the Gunnison River on their right, gleaming icily in
the starshine.

At first Lake City was only a cluster of warm yellow lights,
an island of warmth in the night.

Then it was dark buildings, wood houses, the bulk of a
summer riding stable. Voices, the thud of feet hurrying along
the sidewalk. Music: a jukebox in the Chuck Wagon, muffled
by the walls.

Wood smoke curling fragrantly in the night air.

Wes felt his palms sweating. *God, I'm glad to be back,* he
thought. And then: *But I'm scared stiff.*

Arvon and Nlesine stuck close by his side.

They crept up through shadows, between two wagon wheels.

. . .

"Easy does it," whispered Arvon.

"Yeah," said Wes nervously. "Easy does it."

chapter 18

HE GOT THEM THROUGH IT SOMEHOW.

First there was the meeting with Jim Walls, the salty manager of the Pine Motel. He wasn't ever likely to forget Jim's look of utter astonishment at the sight of Doc Chase: a bearded, skinny, bedraggled wreck of a man. Jim stared at him as though he were Rip Van Winkle, then he insisted on feeding him and giving him a drink—which Wes used to good advantage.

Wes had been stopping with Jim for a number of years, and knew him well enough to fend off his questions. Jim accepted his check for five hundred dollars and obviously felt that Wes had run off with some girl and gotten her into what was locally referred to as motel trouble. He promised not to phone Jo, and Wes took him at his word.

He was acutely aware of Nlesine watching him through the window.

Next day he bought some simple clothes for Arvon and Nlesine, and found a man with a 1938 Ford he was willing to sell for three hundred dollars cash.

And so it was that on the sixteenth of November, with a cold sun staring out of a blue-white sky, they ground up the twisted road across Slumgullion Pass in an old Ford. Arvon and Nlesine crowded in beside him in the front seat, their faces worried and drawn.

It's like a dream to me, Wes thought, *but how strange it all must be to them! An alien world, an alien time, an alien city at the end of the road. And Lortas, not even a light in the sky, spinning toward death, waiting for a visit that would never come.*

But for him—

Jo, and home.

He tried to coax more speed out of the car, without success. He had to keep it in second for a long time, and Lake City was gone, and on either side the world dropped away into pine-marked canyons of sugary snow.

It was a curiously prosaic trip.

Wes settled down into the routine of driving, and even found himself worrying because the car used so much oil. He was involved in an immense problem, he knew that. One day historians might say that the destiny of the human race rode with them in this old car, and it could very well be true. If they ever made a movie of it, Wes was certain that he and Nlesine and Arvon would speak grandiloquent lines about Man and Civilization and Stars. Every police car they saw would be a threat, eyes would regard them suspiciously as they drove.

In actuality, their main problem was where to find a decent meal. They picked up 66 at Gallup, and although New Mexico and Arizona had many charms good food was not among them. They endured a series of grease-bound cheeseburgers, they drank gallons of coffee that was indistinguishable from the

159

battery acid in the car, and they stared without fascination at the fungoid growths of "trading posts" that dotted the desert, offering real-for-sure Indian tom-toms for only a dollar apiece.

Nlesine ventured the observation that perhaps this was a primitive part of the planet and Wes a savage who just hadn't heard about the spaceships and what not on the other side of the pond.

In their khaki shirts and jeans and light jackets, Nlesine and Arvon looked less alien than ever. And, like Wes, they seemed to live mainly for the shower at the end of the day.

It was hard to remember the impersonal forces at work in the universe around them, forces that would touch Earth as well as Lortas if Earth didn't blow herself up before then. The world of the present, of stale candy bars and filter-tip cigarettes and soft drinks in gas stations, was too immediate.

Wes was worried about money. He was not a rich man, and five hundred bucks would put a very perceptible dent in his checking account. How could these men ever pay him back?

He laughed aloud.

Five hundred dollars. Would he give that much to save his world? Would he, voluntarily?

Well, five hundred dollars was a lot of money.

It was easier to let someone else do the worrying. What was the future to him?

Maybe, he thought, *maybe. Maybe that's why man becomes an extinct animal.*

They went through Needles.

"So this is California," Nlesine said, unimpressed. "It looks just like Arizona."

"It gets different," Wes assured him.

They drove on.

Los Angeles sprawls out like an octopus, extending tentacles of gaudy hamburger stands and fuming automobiles for miles toward the north, the south, and the east. Westward lies the sea, and one has the decided feeling that in time that, too, will be straddled by floating housing units and department stores built like pyramids.

There is no abrupt transition from desert to city. It is only that the towns get closer and closer together—Welcome to West Orange Orchard and Gracious Living YOU Can Afford—and then they are all one big city, and that is Los Angeles.

At one point the road goes over a rise, and you can look down into the basin that holds the bulk of Los Angeles. You can't actually *see* the city, of course: all you see is a gray pall of fog, mist, smoke, and that special urban effluvium called smog.

"You mean people live in that without face masks?" asked Nlesine in genuine astonishment.

"I'm afraid so. It isn't so obvious when you're right down in it; you have to get above it to get the full visual appeal."

"Incredible," Arvon said, taking out his pocket handkerchief and holding it over his mouth with what he hoped was a casual manner.

Wes tooled the car along without thinking very much about it. The traffic was heavy, but nothing compared to what it was on a Sunday. He sensed the admiration of his companions, both of whom clearly expected to die at any moment, and he responded to it by driving with an elaborate casualness.

He took them in by way of Union Station, where they picked up the Hollywood Freeway. He edged out into a river of cars and kept to the far right lane because his old automobile couldn't compete in the eternal speed and endurance contests in the center speed tracks. They hurtled out of downtown Los Angeles—that gray jungle left behind to rot when the city exploded toward the Valley and Santa Monica and a myriad of other destinations—and rode the bedlam toward Hollywood.

In a surprisingly short time he cut over to Sunset Boulevard and drove down the wide, curving street in the general direction

161

of Westwood. The character of the place changed drastically now. Mainly it smelled of money.

It was a typical Los Angeles day: cool but not cold, moist and yet not exactly humid. The sun was vaguely visible through the haze, and everywhere you looked there were huge yards choked with brilliant green foliage and dotted with clumps of bright red flowers. The houses, set back at varying distances from the road depending on how much money the owner had, tended toward white Spanish castles and long, low ranch buildings.

There were old ladies seated at booths along the road selling maps that would direct the young at heart and infantile in mind to genuine homes which belonged to real live movie stars—or had belonged to them last week when the current map had been printed.

There were more cars than they had seen on the highway from Colorado to Arizona. All kinds of cars: sedate old black sedans driven by Retired Couples, junk heaps piloted defiantly by the very young or the very poor, brand-new gleaming vehicles with brand-new gleaming Successful Men at the wheels, buglike foreign sports cars weaving in and out of traffic, their goggled drivers ignoring mere stock cars with a vast superiority.

There.

Wes's hands tightened on the wheel.

He stopped at the light on Beverly Glen. If he turned right, toward the Valley, he would be home in five minutes.

Jo.

"Keep going straight ahead, Wes," Arvon said quietly.

The light changed. Grimly Wes stayed on Sunset.

"Where to, gentlemen?" he asked, his voice tight.

"Tourist court," Nlesine said. "Easy does it, Wes—as soon as we find out what we have to know, you can go home and forget all about us. That's a promise."

Arvon looked at Nlesine sharply, then smiled a little.

"Does Wyik know about that?" Wes asked.

Nlesine shrugged. "You escaped."

Wes felt a glow of warmth. Again his mind seethed with contradictions. These men had held him prisoner—and yet, damn it, he was on their side.

The trouble was, he saw suddenly, that he was between two worlds. He was not a part of the mission that had brought the men from Lortas to Earth. And, oddly, he was not quite a part of this world around him either, although he had spent years of his life here.

Somehow *he* had become the alien—and it was not a pleasant feeling.

They passed the black and white sign that pointed toward the University of California at Los Angeles. Turn left there and he would wind up in Westwood Village, where his office was. God, he probably didn't have a patient left any more. If he walked in the door, would Miss Hill still be there, as always?

He stayed on Sunset, stopped again for a light at Sepulveda. He looked around him, at the cars, the houses, the trees, the hustle. There was a newspaper—the *Mirror-News,* not the *Times*—in an orange serve-yourself stand on the corner. He could read the big black headline: RUSSIA SAYS MAYBE. Maybe what? He could even see a photo of some blonde in the left-hand corner. Married? Divorced? Murdered?

The light changed.

He went on, up the hill.

And suddenly the city around him seemed to change. The green lawns and trees became sand, the buildings collapsed and were only steel skeletons fingering the sky. Sand drifted everywhere, tough weeds grew out of sidewalks, the street pavement was cracked and concrete slabs stuck up like dominoes.

Silence, emptiness.

Wind and sand.

Death.

Oh, he knew what he was seeing. It was the world of Centaurus Four, seen through Arvon's eyes. Yes, and hundreds of other worlds that he had never heard of. Worlds of men that had once lived and laughed and brawled as this city blared thoughtlessly around him now.

Wes shivered and came back from reality. Not *to* reality—*from* reality.

He looked at Arvon and Nlesine beside him, and knew that they, too, were seeing Los Angeles as it would one day be. They, too, knew that today was just an early scene in the first act of the tragedy of man.

Why, why had they come too early?

Wes's own problems faded away, a drop in a bucket to be poured into the ocean. He *knew* somehow that this world, this Earth, would survive to master space. And then Earth would find only death around her in the universe, and Earth would count herself unique, and in time Earth would stagnate and die, an isolated island, unable to find her counterpart on Lortas that could give her life forever. . . .

"Turn in there," Arvon said quietly.

Wes started, reached for the lever to turn on his left taillight, then remembered where he was. He stuck out his arm for a turn and pulled into the driveway of a plush motel just off Sunset, still a half mile or so from the Pacific.

The car stopped.

They spent two weeks at the motel, and Wes was never alone.

Arvon and Nlesine took turns going out; sometimes they took Wes along, but not often, for there was always the chance that he would be recognized.

Somewhere Nlesine got some money. He didn't say how he had gotten it, and Wes never asked him. Nlesine blossomed out in a neat charcoal suit, while Arvon merely looked uncomfortable in a moderately clashing sport coat and slacks.

One motel room is much like another. They are fine for spending the night, and there had been a time, with Jo, when Wes had enjoyed them. But two weeks is a long time. He studied the three trite paintings—a rose, a boy examining a bandage, a pallid sunset—and memorized the pattern in the bedspreads. After that he fed the TV set with quarters, and he was not amused.

He supposed that the people on Centaurus Four might have watched such programs just before the world went bang.

There was nothing particularly mysterious about what Arvon and Nlesine were doing. They went to various libraries and looked things up. They bought magazines, particularly news magazines. They made appointments by hook or crook with various technical men, and talked to them guardedly. They made notes.

Nlesine discovered a lending library in a drugstore. He checked out novels and leafed through them rapidly. He was not reassured by an endless series of stories about sadists, supermen, and crafty business executives.

"Is your world *really* like this?" he asked.

Wes shrugged. "Some of it. Not all of it, I hope."

There was nothing at all dramatic about it. They ate three meals a day, got enough sleep, and worked steadily. They made a mountain of notes.

But, gradually, the inevitable became the obvious.

Arvon had dark circles under his eyes.

Nlesine got more and more sarcastic.

On the second day of December, Arvon threw a book at the wall.

"I give up," he said.

"It looks bad to Nlesine."

Wes sat on the bed and stared at his hands. "I tried to tell you."

Arvon paced the floor. "There aren't any magic outs. This world hasn't got manned spaceships, and won't have for a hundred years. It may be two centuries before they hit on an interstellar drive. We're whipped."

Nlesine turned to Wes. "I think you're on our side, Wes. I

165

don't think you'll turn us in for kidnaping, or whatever you want to call it. I promised you we'd turn you loose if we couldn't find anything. We've found nothing, in spades. The only thing we're gambling with now is our lives." He grinned wryly. "Hell, man, why don't you go see your family?"

Wes trembled, got himself under control. "How about you?"

Nlesine shrugged. "We're licked, friend. Any way you cut it, we're not going back to Lortas. I don't believe anyone will listen to us, but I suppose Wyik will try to tell people here about our world and what brought us here. They'll laugh—it'll be great material for comedians. But if we get enough publicity, perhaps someone will remember, someday—when they find out what's waiting for them above the sky." He paused. "Me, I guess I'll find myself some comely wench and see if I can write a novel about the future. It'll stink, of course—a man has to have roots, and mine aren't here. Silly to worry about that now, isn't it?"

Suddenly Wes didn't care. Jo filled his mind, Jo and home and things he understood. He was hungry for them, and he wanted to forget all about space and doom and all the rest of it.

He hardly remembered saying good-by.

He just walked out, climbed in the car, and headed back up Sunset Boulevard.

It was that simple.

He didn't think, he just drove.

And the city was a song around him: *Jo, Jo, Jo.* . . .

166

chapter 19

BEVERLY GLEN IS A CURIOUS, CONTRADICTORY STREET, AND yet it is typical of Los Angeles. From Pico to Wilshire it is a fairly featureless patchwork of identical apartment houses. From Wilshire to Sunset it anticipates Bel-Air Road by featuring spacious lawns, banks of flowers complete with Japanese gardeners, and expensive, dull houses. After the jog at Sunset its character changes sharply.

Coming from the direction of the ocean, Wes turned left on Beverly Glen, joining the steady stream of cars that wound up the hill toward the Valley.

From the moment that he turned, he was home. He smiled, responding to the street he had selected for the arena of his life. Jo had never liked it, and he could see why—it was a crazy street.

But it was his kind of a place.

There wasn't a great deal of money on this part of Beverly Glen, but there was a lot of imagination. More than that, there was variety, the missing ingredient in Los Angeles, where Wes had observed everyone trying so hard to be different that they all wound up looking exactly alike.

There were weird balconies sticking out over the narrow

167

road, there were garages fixed up as studio apartments, there was a modest wood house with a rock castle tower. There were modern all-glass-and-redwood homes, where people seemed to live in shower baths and sometimes pulled the curtain and sometimes didn't, and there were dumps rented to college kids for seventy-five dollars a month.

It was the *feel* of the place that Wes liked. It was shady and reasonably quiet, and there was a surprising amount of open hillside, still beautiful because the landscape experts hadn't gotten to it yet. Wes often had deer come into his back yard, and rabbits and wonderful greenish hummingbirds that buzzed through the sprinkler sprays. And there were always friendly California lizards scrabbling around in the leaves.

He could have driven it with his eyes shut, even in the old Ford. He had a strange feeling that he had never been away, that he had just gone to the office as usual and was coming home for dinner.

There were no spaceships on Beverly Glen.

He passed a sign painted in the middle of the street in big red letters. It said: BILL REMEMBER JIMMY'S BICYCLE.

He grinned, wondered who Bill was, and could almost see him snapping his fingers, turning around, and rushing back somewhere for Jimmy's bike.

It was a good street.

He turned off on one of those streets that seem to go straight up the side of the mountain, ground along in second for two minutes, and turned right into a driveway half hidden by a brilliant green hedge.

He was home.

Wes felt tears in his eyes and damned himself for a sentimental fool. He stopped the car. He got out, smelling the green-wet air as though it had been created for him alone. There—he saw his own car in the carport. And the rock and redwood house —nothing sensational, maybe, but it was his, or would be with a few more payments.

168

He listened, heard nothing but a dog yapping down below.

Jo was alone.

He ran across the dichondra to the front door, slipped his key in the lock, pushed it open.

He glanced quickly through the kitchen, the living room, the semi-enclosed brick patio. Then he hurried down the hall, excited as a kid, and opened the bedroom door.

"Jo," he said.

And stopped.

Norman Scott got up off the edge of the bed, his face whiter than the sheets.

"Wes," whispered Jo. "Oh my God, *Wes*."

She covered herself, hid her face in the pillow, sobbing.

"Look here, old man," Norman said, talking very fast. "Look here, old man." He ran out of gas, stopped.

Wes stood absolutely still. His stomach tied itself into knots and his head was spinning. He couldn't see. He felt nothing, nothing at all.

"I—we thought you were dead," Norman whispered. "No word, no nothing. What were we to think? We didn't know, couldn't know——"

"Shut up," Wes said. He said it softly, without anger. He didn't want to hear Norm's voice. That was all.

Jo didn't look at him.

"I'd better be going," Norm said inanely.

"Yes. You'd better go."

He didn't see him leave, but he was alone with his wife.

He touched her bare shoulder, not ungently. It felt cold, like marble. "Shut up," he said.

Jo choked into silence. She lay there trembling. She still didn't look at him.

"You love him?" Wes asked. It was an empty question; he didn't care.

"Yes. No. I don't know." Jo's voice was so muffled he could hardly understand her.

Wes fumbled out a cigarette, lit it. His hands were steady. He looked around. The bed—he remembered how they had shopped for a mattress that wouldn't sag with his weight, yet wasn't too hard for her. Pale blue wallpaper. Closet with his clothes in it, her dresses. A slip hanging on the bathroom doorknob.

He heard her voice from a long way off: "Where did you go? I was frantic. What could I do? He was so nice to me, so kind. Wes, why did you leave me?" Her voice hardened. "I *told* you never to go off and leave me sitting in that miserable cabin! Was I supposed to wait all winter?" She began sobbing again. "Oh, Wes—my God——"

Wes wasn't listening.

He looked at her. She had lost a little weight, her blonde hair was gold on the pillow.

"Stiff upper lip and all that," he heard himself saying.

"What?"

"Nothing. Adults. Be civilized, sophisticated."

She looked at him now.

"No, I'm not crazy." He smiled without humor, wondering what she would think if he told her where he had been, what had happened. Then he shrugged.

It didn't matter now.

He was a stranger here. This was not his home, this was not the woman he had married. Like all the rest of his life, this too had been taken from him.

He was alone in the room, with a stranger.

Jo climbed out of bed, shivered into a robe, pushed back her hair. "Give me a cigarette, Wes."

He didn't even hear her.

"I ought to beat the hell out of you or something, but it isn't worth the effort."

"Please give me a cigarette."

"You'll be taken care of. You haven't a thing to worry about."

"Wes, I don't understand you."

"Never mind."

"Wes, I'm going to call Horace. You need a doctor. You look—awful. Look, can't we talk this over? This isn't the Middle Ages. We're sensible men and women."

Wes turned and walked out the door.

"Wes!"

He walked out of an alien house into alien sunshine.

He felt nothing, saw nothing.

He got in the old Ford, backed into the street, and drove into nowhere.

When he came back to himself, he was driving on Olympic Boulevard and he was sobbing. He had a cigarette in his mouth and it had burned down too far; it seared his lip. He spat it out the window without touching it with his fingers.

He watched an intersection go by. Vermont Avenue. Practically downtown. He had no idea how he had gotten there and didn't care. He made three right turns and then a left, and he was headed the other way, toward Santa Monica.

He stopped at a liquor store and bought three fifths of White Horse Scotch.

"Gonna have a party?" the man asked.

"Yeah. My debut."

Back in the car. To Beverly Glen again, and over to Sunset. Down Sunset in a crush of cars.

The motel.

He got out, knocked on the door of the cabin.

No answer.

He knocked again.

"It's Wes," he said. "Open the door, damn it."

The door opened slowly, and there was Nlesine with a gun in his hand.

"Paralyze me," he said. "Please."

Nlesine eyed him, looked up and down for policemen, and let him in.

"I was afraid you'd be gone," Wes said.

"You took our car, pal." Then Nlesine noticed his face. "Wes. What's wrong, man?"

"The world just ended ahead of schedule. I hope you would like to get drunk, because I hate to drink alone."

Then Wes ran out of words. He fell on the bed. He couldn't even cry.

Arvon closed the door carefully.

He touched Wes's shoulder.

He spoke in his own language, but what he said could be understood anywhere, in any tongue.

"Come on," Nlesine said when the silence was too much to bear. "Open the bottle, Arvon."

Wes's glasses had fallen off, but he didn't need them for what he was seeing.

The scotch went down like warm oil, but he was cold, cold as the emptiness between the worlds.

They went after the first bottle with a certain steady determination, but it was evening before they polished it off.

From that point their course was clear before them.

They started in on the second bottle.

Wes told them what had happened. He tried to be very hard-boiled and unconcerned about it, but he wasn't fooling anyone, least of all himself.

While he talked, he thought: *I wonder what happened to Arvon and Nlesine back on Lortas. This is what drives a man outside himself, even to the stars. It isn't high-minded, it isn't abstract. This is what it is: fear and loneliness that can never be forgotten, no matter how far you go, no matter how long you travel. . . .*

"A toast, gentlemen," Nlesine said. "To the rescuers of the Universe, the heroes of the Cosmos!"

They had one on that.

They similarly honored the girls on Lortas (no finer brand on any planet), Happy Wyik, and red-blooded American boys.

They got on famously, and Wes began to feel slightly better. But then the inevitable happened: Arvon and Nlesine began to reminisce about old times. Soon they were laughing hysterically, slapping each other on the back, lost in long-ago events in which Wes had no part.

He was alone again.

He was also sobering up. The scotch just made him sick at his stomach. He sat on the bed and listened and stared at the wall.

He looked at his life.

He didn't like it.

He was not a fool. He knew that he had built up too rosy a picture of Jo while he was lying in that cave. Jo hadn't been like that, not for many years. But a man had to believe in something, had to have a home. . . .

Sure, it had been his fault, too. He had been crazy about Jo, he'd had to have her. He had known she didn't want his kind of life, but he hadn't cared—then.

Oh, you're a great man, Wes. Three cheers for you.

He remembered Cincinnati, himself as a boy. Winter snow and sliding down those crazy hills, dodging the trees, coming up *smack* against black logs. Going back to the house, fighting to get his wet shoes off, the way his numb feet tingled in the warmth. Summer nights, hot and muggy, and you let the fan blow on your sweat and listened to the train whistles over in Norwood, it seemed a million miles away, and a million years. . . .

Spring and baseball, every afternoon, playing until it was too dark to see the ball down in the empty lot at the end of the street. Woods and secret green trails, swinging on vines over the creek, catching crawdads under the rocks. September and football and knowing you were good, knowing the girls were watching you, the wonderful fearful mysterious girls, and dreaming that somehow, someday, you would marry one of those girls

173

and then, of course, it would be an orgy every night and life would be swell forever.

It all seemed pale after that. College was a gray blur of coffee and greasy eggs and dreary singsong teachers. He remembered one old duffer reading a poem by Sandburg, then mumbling, "Is that a poem? If that's a poem, I'm Hercules!" And Tom was going to dress up in a leopard skin and come to class and leap up and say, "It is a poem, and I am Hercules!" Only he never had.

Med school was better, and the research had caught his interest. The lab had excited him—God, he used to work all night. But Jo wanted money, and that had meant the runny noses and the office, the millions and billions of runny noses, the endless afternoons. . . .

Was he different? Was he unique? Or did this happen to all American men? He tried to think of men he knew who were happy, really happy. It seemed that as soon as you got to know a man well you discovered that he hated his work, or tolerated it, and wanted to get away—where?

And then Colorado, and the fantastic weeks in the vault where five men had slept for fifteen thousand years. And the story, the wonderful story of a ship that had touched the stars, searching, searching. . . .

It had been the most interesting thing that had ever happened to him. And now even that had ended in failure, and that failure was a personal thing, and here they were, three bums in a motel slugging down the booze.

Nlesine almost finished the second bottle and smacked his lips. There was still a drop or two in it, but hardly enough to bother about. He put the cap back on tightly, though. "Save it for later," he muttered, and opened the third fifth.

Wes suddenly got up off the bed.

He stared at the two men with him and he was cold-sober.

And hopeful.

Maybe——

"Wait a minute," he whispered. *"Wait a minute."*

chapter 20

THERE WAS BLACK COFFEE, ARGUMENT, AND MORE BLACK coffee.

There was restless, nervous sleep.

And then, after a morning tug of war with fried eggs and bacon and still more black coffee, there was only one thing to do. They had to get back to Colorado, and fast.

That same afternoon they drove out Sepulveda to the International Airport and caught a twin-engined plane for Denver. It was a choppy flight, and did their stomachs no good. At Denver they rented a car and drove to Lake City, coming into it behind Slumgullion Pass, which was pretty well iced over.

It was a tough climb up the mountain along the black, icy stream, but they hardly noticed the snow and the wind and the bitter cold. Numb and red-faced and excited, they clambered into the rock shelter and rapped on the port.

There was no answer.

"It's us, damn it!" Nlesine hollered out in Lortan. "Spring is here, and we knew you'd want to go pick wild flowers. Come on out, you crusty old men!"

The port opened slowly, and there were Wyik and Hafij and Tsriga, guns ready.

"Fine welcome," Nlesine observed, moving into the vault. "Your joy at our return touches us deeply."

Wyik caught his shoulder. "Don't play with us, man! What did you find out? Quick!"

"We can't build a ship," Arvon said. "It's impossible."

Wyik's face fell.

Tsriga sat down on the floor.

Hafij didn't bat an eye.

"Hold off awhile on the suicides, though," Nlesine said quietly. "I think we've got a chance—and we can thank Wes for thinking of something we all stupidly overlooked." He grinned. "Yeah, the alien nobody would trust. *Him.*"

Wyik turned to Wes. "But what——"

"Wait." Arvon hurried over to the five niches cut into the rock wall. He fell to his knees, pawing through the pebbles and dirt and twigs that had accumulated.

"I don't see it," he whispered.

"Fine housekeepers," Nlesine muttered, and joined him.

"It's *got* to be——"

"Hold it. Here it is."

Nlesine held it up, and it was just as they had known it would be.

They sat and talked and hoped and ate a whopping meal of venison; the newcomers relished the venison more than the three men who had been eating it for weeks.

Then they slept the sleep of the exhausted.

Next morning Wes and Arvon and Nlesine went back down the mountain trail, their prize wrapped in a handkerchief and pinned in Nlesine's coat pocket.

Two days later they were back in Los Angeles.

That was where Wes got down to business.

The arrangements were not easy, but Wes Chase was almost happy as he worked. For once he had come up with something he could be proud of, and for once he was doing something that really interested him.

Not by himself, of course—but it was his brain that set it in motion.

For a while he forgot about Jo, forgot about everything but the problem at hand. This was his kind of a problem—and it could be licked.

It took them the better part of two years.

Wes had friends from his endocrine research days who were now strategically spotted in the big labs. They helped carry the ball, and the whole thing was virtually a routine performance for a trained team of researchers.

It cost Wes money, of course, but he didn't care. He cashed in his pile of stocks and bonds with something like relish.

The steps were the usual ones:

First, a detailed qualitative analysis.

Second, a delicate quantitative one.

Finally, a lengthy process of purification, repeated tests with drug derivatives, experiments on white mice and rhesus monkeys.

It was tough going, but no miracles were required.

It boiled down to this: *It was impossible for today's technology to manufacture a spaceship out of vague mental blueprints. Even had the ship still existed, many problems would have been almost insoluble—and the ship was dust and less than dust after fifteen thousand years. But the substance that had put the men from Lortas to sleep in the first place was a relatively simple compound. As Arvon had told Wes, the injection that produced suspended animation was an extract from the lymphoid tissue of hibernating mammals, like the woodchucks, in combination with an absorbent of vitamin D and insulin and some common drug derivatives. If the labs had a sample to go by, no matter how small, the stuff could be synthesized. And Wyik had not used quite all of the drug. He had resealed a few drops in the self-refrigerating duraglass container and dropped it on the floor. There it had stayed, preserved at a temperature close to absolute zero, while centuries marched by. . . .*

The wonder was that none of them had thought of the possibility until Wes had seen Nlesine recap the scotch bottle with a few drops still left in it. After that, with Wes's own earlier experience in endocrine research as a trigger, the result was almost a foregone conclusion. The seasonal changes in the functioning of the pituitary glands of hibernating animals were well known to him, and offered a ready-made excuse when he went to the labs with his problem.

In less than two years they had it.

"You'd better be careful with this stuff, Wes," Garvin Berry, in charge of the project, said when they were through. "It knocks our lab animals out like a light."

"We'll watch our step, Garv," Wes assured him.

It was as simple as that.

The three of them had taken a somewhat uninspired apartment in Santa Monica, but Wes did not go directly back to Arvon and Nlesine. He had something he had to do first.

The priceless drug, sealed in a thick glass bottle, was on the front seat next to him as he drove. It looked oddly commonplace, even to Wes—with a little imagination it became only a bottle of milk; he had picked it up at a Westwood grocery, and now he was bringing it home to Jo . . .

But it was a bottle of milk that had set him back many thousands of dollars.

And there was no more Jo.

And no more home.

He had gotten used to it, he supposed. There was no more pain, only a hollow emptiness somewhere inside of him where his life used to be. He did not blame Jo, or Norm. He had made a fizzle out of his life without any help from them.

If he had only been man enough to do what he wanted to do instead of what Jo thought she wanted him to do.

If he had insisted on children.

If he had taken charge of his own life while there was still time.

If, if, if.

The hell with it. His hands tightened on the steering wheel. At least he had not failed in this. He had done one thing in his life that was worth doing. And he wasn't through yet.

Half unconsciously he began the pilgrimage.

He drove through a summer haze out along the coast highway. The road was crawling with cars. The sandy beaches were littered with people soaking up the sun. The hamburger and hot-dog stands were doing a roaring business. And the private cottages that lined the ocean, the cottages that all winter were so brown and damp and desolate, had their windows open and cars in their garages.

He pulled in at the Point and went inside.

"Doc!" One of the waiters hurried over to him, smiling. "Haven't seen you in years. How's Mrs. Chase?"

"Fine, fine." How strange to be called Doc again! Were the pieces of his life still scattered here, waiting to be picked up? "Bring me a scotch and soda out on the balcony, would you please?"

"Right away, Doc. Good to have you back."

He went out on the balcony and seated himself in the shade there. He could hear the water below him, hissing and murmuring as it curled in on the beach and sucked around the black rocks. He looked out over the ocean, blue and sparkling under a clear sky. There were fishing boats out there, black dots in the sunshine, but mostly there was loneliness, and peace.

He watched the gulls wheeling over the shallows, nosing down after fish. Along the shore line some pipers were earnestly

179

examining the wet sand, then skittering back to avoid the breakers when they folded in.

He took off his glasses and closed his eyes, nursing his drink. The murmur of the sea was infinitely soothing. He and Jo had come here many times in that other life, had gotten tight, laughed, done crazy things. If only a man could go back, he thought—back to childhood springs, back to light hearts and carefree nights that would last forever . . .

If.

He put his glasses back on and stared, almost hypnotized, at the sea. *We're all aliens here on the land,* he thought. *We're fish out of water, flopping on the rocks.*

"Wes old boy," he said aloud, "you are one cheerful bastard."

He paid for his drink and left a much bigger tip than necessary.

He climbed in his car and drove back along the beach, up the hill to Santa Monica, then out Wilshire to Westwood. He found an empty parking space near his office, put two pennies in the meter, and just sat in his car looking. He had let Miss Hill go, of course, but some obscure impulse had led him to keep up the office rent. He could read the black and gold sign outside the building: WESTON J. CHASE, M.D.

His middle name was Jasper, and he hated it. He remembered when Jo had had a fake sign made up once as a gag: W. JASPER CHASE, M.D. He smiled. God, that was a long time ago.

He didn't know how long he stayed there, but he noticed with a start that the meter was red. He drove off: down Olympic to Beverly Glen.

The boundaries of my life.

He made the jog at Sunset, where Bel-Air started, and drove along through the quiet shade of Beverly Glen. He looked for the sign that had reminded Bill to remember Jimmy's bicycle, but it was gone, of course. He turned up his hill, angled off into what had been his driveway.

He stopped the car, got out. He stood half-hidden by his hedge. He could have been seen from the house if anyone had been looking. He didn't move, neither calling attention to his presence nor concealing it.

He wondered whether he wanted to be seen.

The air was wet and green, and the dichondra was as smooth as a golf course. Jo was keeping the yard in good shape. The rock and redwood house was peaceful in the afternoon shadows.

Was she there?

He had seen her several times in the past two years, but only with their lawyer. She was well taken care of, and she had seemed happy.

Glad to be rid of me, probably.

No, that was unjust. He knew Jo. She would never admit that she had been hurt, even as he had been hurt. She would have given no sign to him.

He saw himself walking up to the door. She answered it, not looking her best. She brushed back her blonde hair, wished she had remembered to put on lipstick.

"Wes."

"Jo, I've been thinking—about lots of things. Could I come in for a while?"

She hesitated, only a moment.

"You're alone, Jo?"

"Of course, silly. Come on in, Wes."

He would go in and then—what?

Would she take him back? Did he want her back? Oh, the attraction was still there, and he hadn't been with her for two years. Just walk up to the door . . .

Could they begin again?

Wes knew the answer to that one. They could begin again— you could always begin again. But how would it end?

He knew the answer to that one, too. He was what he was, and she was what she was. It hadn't worked, not really, and it never would.

He stood there by the hedge, unmoving. *You fool,* he thought. *You're waiting for her to come out to you.*

If she saw him, she gave no sign.

He didn't go in.

The shadows lengthened and it was night. He saw stars sprinkled in the sky above him.

"Good-by, old girl," he said.

He got back in the car and drove away.

This time when he got to Santa Monica he went to the apartment where Arvon and Nlesine were waiting for him.

"Ho!" said Nlesine, tossing down a novel he was reading. "Did you get ambushed or something?"

"Or something," Wes admitted.

Arvon took the heavy glass bottle and gave it a smacking kiss. "You got it!"

"It's ready. Garv says it's an exact duplicate of the stuff we gave him to work on. I hope he's right."

"He's *got* to be right," Arvon said.

"The incurable optimist," Nlesine muttered, rubbing his balding head. "It's probably not as good as Nembutal."

They fixed themselves a dinner, with Nlesine showing off his new-found skill with spaghetti. It was good, and so was the wine, but they were all unusually subdued.

This was the end of the road.

"It's a crazy business," Arvon said finally. "We woke up after fifteen thousand years in a rock vault in Colorado, just when you happened to crawl into that shelter to get out of the storm. There probably hadn't been another human being in there since we went to sleep. And I had to grab you and scare you half to death and foul up your life for you."

"I did that for myself," Wes put in.

"Maybe. But there we were—and after fifteen thousand years we were still too early! I'm convinced now that Earth is the world we've been seeking—you are so much like us, Wes, that only almost identical cultural strains could have produced our

182

two peoples. But we had failed until you came up with your bright idea. It looks like you saved us, Wes—and saved far more than that. But——" He paused.

"But you still get the short end of the stick," Nlesine finished.

"I think you're giving me credit for more altruism than I have," Wes said slowly. "I didn't do all this just out of the goodness of my heart. I didn't do it for that neat abstraction called the world, either. I'm a selfish animal, gentlemen."

"Ah. You have a price." Nlesine grinned as though reassured.

"Yes."

They waited.

Wes took a deep breath. "I'm going with you," he said.

chapter 21

THERE WAS NO HURRY NOW, SO THEY DROVE THROUGH THE Southwest to Colorado. They traveled at night in Arizona and New Mexico, and stopped in air-conditioned tourist courts by day.

Lake City was enjoying its annual rush season as the trout fishermen came in, and in truth the place *did* have a far livelier air about it than it had in the winter.

They left the car at the Pine Motel, with a note to Jim Walls, who had cashed Wes's check when he had first come back down the mountain. Then they hoofed it through the delightful Colorado sunshine, beside the blue waters of the swift-flowing Gunnison. The mountains loomed around them, inviting them with the enchantment of distance and the clean green of pine stands.

They turned off the main road at the creek, followed the tiny path into the brush. There were no cars parked along the stream, and that was good.

Up through the valley of green and gold, with the water chuckling and gurgling on their right. Even as they scrambled up the mountain trail, Wes caught himself eying one or two pools of dark water and imagining the trout that lurked in them fanning their fins. . . .

They climbed on, past the cool pines and slender aspens, their boots treading on jungles of fern and flower. Then they left the spruces behind them and there was no more timber.

By the time they turned off at the shelter, they were good and tired, and Wes was worried. What would Wyik say?

Up into the rock shelter.

The port opened to receive them.

They were back in the vault.

Nlesine held up the thick glass bottle triumphantly. "We're in!" he said.

"We have Wes to thank for it," Arvon said.

Tsriga and even Hafij were smiling oddly secretive smiles.

Wes cleared his throat. "I came back with them," he said, and then stopped. *That's obvious enough, you idiot.* "I came back because I—because I hoped that you wouldn't mind if——"

"Shut up," Wyik said, not unkindly.

"What?"

"Are you blind, Wes?"

Wes looked around him, bewildered. Everything looked about the same. The untidy floor, the wood for the fireplace, the odds and ends, the niches cut into the far wall——

Wait a minute.

There had only been five niches before: Wyik, Arvon, Nlesine, Tsriga, Hafij.

Now there were six.

Wyik grabbed his hand, and the Captain's face relaxed into

a rare smile. "We hoped you'd come along, Wes," he said. "After all, you're one of us now."

Wes found it hard to speak.

It wasn't the niche itself, it wasn't even the great adventure that the niche implied. No, it was more than that.

He was wanted. *God,* he thought, *somebody likes me, somebody wants to have me around.*

It was a good feeling.

Damn it, I am NOT going to cry like a baby!

"Thanks," he said. "Thanks very much."

Then he walked away, out of the vault toward the glacial lake that glinted in the pale sun, because this was a good time for a man to be alone with his thoughts.

The night before they started, Wes was sitting out under the stars, shivering a little in the high, thin wind, listening to some animal snort through the brush below him.

Arvon climbed out of the rock shelter and joined him.

"We used to sit out under the stars like this on Lortas," he said. "It's hard to think that all the girls you used to know have been dead for fifteen thousand years."

Wes nodded, although it was still hard for him to get used to the idea. "Funny, but I always think of all of you as going *home,* back to the world you left—but that's not the way it will be, is it?"

Arvon picked up a pebble and skipped it down toward the invisible animal, which responded with a flurry of movement. "Lortas will still be there unless all the predictions were wrong. But it won't be *our* Lortas—not after fifteen thousand years or so. It's almost as though you had left the Earth at the end of the Stone Age and come back to it today—but it's not quite that bad, actually. Things had slowed down on Lortas before we left, just as they will slow down here after another few hundred years."

"But you'll be strangers, just the same."

186

"We'll all be in the same boat, Wes."

Wes kept talking. He recognized the nervousness in himself, he needed reassurance, needed it badly. *We might never wake up,* he was thinking. *We might wake up and find the Earth a radioactive desert. The odds, the fantastic odds. . . .*

"I think you're missing the point," Arvon said finally. "Sure, we keep talking about odds and statistics and all that. Sure, we were scared the first time—scared that this world would be like the others, all the others scattered through the skies. But, Wes, you *haven't* blown yourselves to bits—and you've had the technology to do it, and the provocation, too. The really incredible thing to me is how much, how very much, this world is like our own. Hell, I'm no more an alien here than you are now—a little different physically, maybe, but not so much that I couldn't walk through the streets of Los Angeles without anyone looking at me twice."

Wes smiled to himself. For all his claims, there were a few things Arvon still didn't know about Earth. "No offense intended," he said, "but I'm afraid most anything could live in Los Angeles unnoticed."

Arvon shrugged. "Okay, true enough. But it's no accident we are as similar as we are, Wes. This world, basically, is Lortas as Lortas was a long time ago. There are differences, important differences, of course. It's those differences that will make a new life possible for both worlds one day, if we can ever get them together. But it's the *similarities* that are important to us now. I *know* that Earth will not destroy herself. I *know* she will develop space travel. I *know* we're not going to fail now."

Wes lit a cigarette. "We have a custom called whistling in the graveyard," he said. "But, thanks, even if it was a whistle."

The two men sat in silence then under the glory of the stars.

Wes looked up at them out into the sea of night. *Sometime I may be out there, out with the suns and the darkness and the silence——*

It was late when they returned to the vault.

187

Wes remembered that other time, when Arvon had carried him into the shelter, when Arvon had been a creature out of a nightmare. It seemed a million years ago.

He did not look back, although he knew he would never see the world that waited at the foot of the mountain path again.

He heard Nlesine snoring lustily as he stretched out on the hard floor.

How strange, how strange that we want a good night's sleep before we sleep for five hundred years. . . .

He slept.

The morning was filled with tense jokes.

They had always been careful to conceal any traces of their presence on the outside, so that was all attended to. They ate a good big breakfast, all of them eating more than they really wanted. After all, lunch was five hundred years away.

They sealed off the vault.

Wes got his hypodermic needle out and cleaned it in alcohol.

He was nervous, but his hands were steady.

"All right, Wes," Wyik said. "Let's get on it. Make absolutely certain that you give us all *exactly* the same dose. And be sure you lie down in the niche before you inject yourself— it hits fast."

Rather self-consciously they all shook hands.

Nobody said, and everyone thought, *What if it doesn't work, what if the lab made a mistake, what if this is the end . . . ?*

Wyik slid into his niche, settled himself.

"All right, Wes," he said again.

Wes cleaned a spot on his arm with cotton dipped in alcohol, opened the heavy glass container, filled the hypo with precisely one cubic centimeter of the drug. The stuff compounded its effect as the dosage was increased, he had to be careful. . . .

He inserted the hypo expertly, pressed the plunger.

Wyik's haunted, desperate eyes clouded, closed, and he slept. Wes stared at him. He didn't seem to be alive, he could see no

188

chest movement. He took his wrist. Yes, there was the pulse, but fading, fading. . . .

"Next," said Nlesine.

Very carefully, forcing himself to concentrate on the job and nothing else, Wes made the rounds.

A corner of his mind refused to be silent.

All of you, all of you, he thought. *You, Wyik, and Nlesine, and Arvon, and Tsriga, and Hafij. You have all lost something, even as I have lost something. What happened in your lives on Lortas that sent you here? A man can be driven only by the springs inside himself. You, Nlesine—were you a good novelist? Were you good enough? You, Arvon—if your life was empty, did you seek to fill it here? Tsriga, you were a boy when you came here, but you will be a man when you return. I hope the next woman will be worthy of you. Hafij, what loneliness made you seek the stars for your home? And, Wyik, strange Wyik, are you too running away? What made the black unrest in your soul?*

It was done.

Wes turned out the tubelights, all except one that he held in his hand. He filled the needle for the last time. Then, smiling a little, he carefully recapped the heavy glass container.

He crawled into his rock cubicle.

The vault was dark and empty around him, the solid rock above him seemed the weight of centuries.

And yet he was not alone. The men who slept in the darkness around him understood. They, too, had lost something, everything, and they, too, were searching. . . .

He injected himself, switched off the light.

Darkness, shadows—

And a greater, softer oblivion.

Sound.

That came first.

189

It curled into his mind like smoke, blue smoke, wood smoke, and it was a voice, talking, whispering . . .

A language he didn't know. Strange. What was it?

Ah! Lortan. He recognized it.

Wyik's voice.

Suddenly, shatteringly, he opened his eyes. Light. It hurt. He blinked, kept them open. He felt the rock under his body, he felt the squeezing heart in his chest, the liquid sluggish in his veins. . . .

"I'm awake." He said it aloud, his voice a croak. "I'm not dead. I'm *awake*."

A hand on his shoulder. Wyik's. "Easy," said the Captain. "Take it slow. There's no hurry. You're all right."

Wes lay still, gathering his strength. He was cold. He felt his chest, and scraps of rotted cloth fell away. *Naked*, he thought. *Me, a nudist.*

He managed a smile.

After a while he crawled out of the niche, stood up. He was lightheaded and thought he was falling, but he recovered himself in time. *Skinny, God, I'm skinny*. Wyik, too, was thin and pale, his eyes feverish in his head.

Hungry.

"Outside," he said. "Have you looked?"

"No. I listened, couldn't hear anything. I was waiting."

One of the others stirred, groaned. Tsriga.

"Let's wait until we can all go," Wyik said.

Wes sat down on the floor, shivering. It was hard to think, hard to come back from the dead. He wondered how Arvon had come out of it so fast that time long ago—how long ago now?

But he was *alive*.

They waited, and when they were all ready Wyik cautiously opened the port.

Light, light and silence.

They went into the rock shelter, looked out.

190

Nothing had changed. Sky, rocks, brush, stream——

Wes felt despair clutch him in an icy fist.

"What's happened? It's all the same. God, didn't the stuff *work?*"

Arvon shook his head. "It was like this before," he said. "A spot like this, high in the mountains—why would it change?"

Whistling in the dark?

They saw no human figure. They heard no animals—no sound at all save a sighing wind.

Dead. The place is dead. Earth, too. . . .

"Wait."

He heard it. They all heard it.

A rumble, as of thunder, far away.

Coming closer.

A blasting roar, a hurricane of sound——

They saw it.

Above them.

A ship, a prodigious ship, a mountain of metal and glass that blotted out the sun. Its shadow crossed them. The thing was immense, so high in the sky, so beautiful—

And it was gone.

Only the thunder remained, rolling over the mountains.

Hafij was crying. "A ship, a spaceship." He said it over and over again, tasting the words on his tongue.

"We made it," Arvon said.

We made it, we made it.

He remembered, they all remembered: *No human culture on record had ever succeeded in finding and establishing friendly relations with another human culture on a different planet. If a world could be found where men were sane, if contacts could be built up between them, if ideas and hopes and dreams could flow from one to the other—*

Then perhaps man might someday be more than just another animal who lost his way. . . .

They paused long enough to drink the cold, clean water from

191

the glacial lake. They laughed and joked and cried, not daring to believe, but having to believe.

They started down the path, the swift mountain stream at their side, running, running—

Past the spruces, the whispering pines, the slender aspens.

Into a warm summer valley, all green and gold, alive with color and the songs of birds.

Toward a new world, a new hope.

Derryoc went with them, and Seyehi, and Lajor, and Kolraq, a smile on his face. Wes felt tears in his eyes. Jo was there too— Jo and the life that had almost been, and never was.

The sunlight was life, and promise.

Wes wasn't thinking about the world, or two worlds, or the universe.

I'm only forty. That's not so old. There is still time for me, time for children and happiness and life. Only forty, only forty, there is still time for me. . . .

They were all moving into the unknown.

No one of them had a home.

But they knew now that the winds of time are patient and blow forever.

This was not the end.

This was the beginning.